A Heart That's Taken

Beyond The Wallace's

Carey Anderson

ISBN:0692346902
ISBN-13:9780692346907

DEDICATION

This one is dedicated to my Diva. Thank you for your constant support and appreciation. I've always enjoyed your enthusiasm for reading, and every book you suggested, I thoroughly enjoyed. I hope you enjoy my contribution to the literary world.

Also, I would like to thank all of my fellow BookTubers who explained to me on YouTube what NaNo WriMo was all about. This challenge was a lot of fun and I got to meet a lot of amazing authors in my area.

Join me on Facebook –
www.facebook.com/careythewriteranderson

Twitter - @CareyTheWriter

Blog - http://careyanderson.blogspot.com

Website – http://www.careythewriteranderson.com

Author Central (Amazon) -
http://www.amazon.com/author/careyanderson

Editorial – Treasures of Joy Editorial

Cover Design: Carey Anderson

Photography by – Carey Anderson

ACKNOWLEDGMENTS

I would like to thank my baby-girl who is my life's ultimate expression of a dream realized. Thank you for sacrificing mommy time so that I could have the time to work some things out on paper.

I would like to thank my Soul Sistah #1 who has been my captivated audience since middle school. Without your love, support, encouragement, and FIRE I never would've completed Volume I or II, etc. Thank you for bringing me laughter when I couldn't get outside of my head.

I would like to thank my Sister-In-Law for taking time out of your busy family life to humor me with a read through of my latest thoughts and expressions. (SS1 & SIL THANK YOU for the trip to St. Helena where we spent the day lost in my imagination. I will never forget it, and it was exactly what I needed. THANK YOU!)

I would like to thank my dear cousin for reassuring me that my little hobby was relatable and entertaining. You are definitely a speed-reader, thank you for taking time out of your busy life to be entertained by my imagination.

I would like to thank last but not least Mrs. Laverne Dyes! Mrs. Dyes the day that you read my short story to my class changed my life. Thank you for giving me a positive outlet for all the angst going on in my life.

Chapter 1

Olivia

"I'm glad you finally came out. Now it's time to make this money, and forget about that loser Montell." My best friend Julia said.

Julia's family is from out here in Georgia. Her family came to California for a short while and that's when we met on the playground. She's always had my back and I hers. When Julia's parents divorced, her mother stayed in California while she had to move back out here with her father. We've kept in contact over the years via letters, occasional phone calls, and videos. Both of our parents had camcorders and we used them to our advantage. Julia is one of the best photographers I know. Well she's the only photographer that I know, but I still know she's the best. She has a wonderful eye for catching light and moments. One of the games we play is "capture that mood." I used to send her songs that I would tape off the radio that I felt described the mood I was in. I'd tell her to capture as many pictures as she could that reflected the mood of that song. When she'd send me pictures, I'd listen to my song again and then we'd go over the pictures. We normally ended up debating about most of them. That's the thing about artistic expression. Sometimes two people will look at the same item and get two TOTALLY different ideas about what the pieces mean. Like what the artist is saying, the whole thing. Most times, we didn't agree, and in the end, we would agree to disagree. I moved out here to escape my sorry excuse for a life. There was no college fund or plans made for me, which never seemed to add up to me. Our house was in a very nice neighborhood in Castro Valley. My mom drives only top of the line cars, and she trades up every so many years. She dresses very nicely from the top of her head to the bottom of her feet. Ms. Roth or the dragon lady as I like to call her, sometimes is always nicely put together. When I graduated from high school, my mother said I needed to get a job and then find a place to live. Since there was nothing holding me in Castro Valley, the city where I grew up, I jumped on the opportunity for a change of scenery. Julia graduated from high school a year early and is in college. She landed a job, which allowed her to maintain an apartment of her own. She told me she was sending for me as soon as I told her that Montell and I broke up. I'm going to the local junior college until I figure out what I'm going to do. I don't know where my life is going, but anything has to be better than this. "Thanks love, here's to new beginnings."

Ahjani

"You are the first person to go to college in our family! I am so proud of you son. Remember to remain focused. Don't let anyone steer you away from what you know is true. Basketball is your ticket in; it's paying for the ride. Remember that you are there to get your **education**. Play well, but don't let go of your Plan B. Even if you make it into the NBA, you could get injured, or never make it off the bench. The list goes on and on. You will be a success not because of that ball you bounce around, but because you will apply the biggest muscle you have on your body." My momma said.

"Thank you momma," I said hugging her.

"Aquilla, stop babying him. I'm proud of you...."

I took my momma by the hand and we walked closer to the gate. "I don't know why you invited him." I looked down on my momma.

"He's your father baby. I don't want to be the reason why you don't have a relationship with him." Her eyes were sad.

"You are my father, you are my momma. He barely paid child support and I only saw him when he could be bothered. I have nothing to say to him." I tried to keep my voice controlled; I didn't want her thinking that my irritation was with her.

"What is wrong with you? I didn't come all the way out here to be treated like this! I can go home!"

"Good, then you should. I didn't invite you here. I don't even know you, but you want to act like we're supposed to have some kind of bonding moment at the airport. Everything I am I owe it to my momma and my sister. You are a stranger to me! Go back to existing on mute as far as I'm concerned." Then I kissed my momma goodbye; I took immense pleasure in knowing that my words hurt him. I boarded my plane feeling like I could finally leave the issues with my father behind me. I finally had the chance to say everything on my heart in those couple of sentences. It felt as good as my sister used to say it would. Here's to a new beginning where I can finally leave all my drama behind me.

As soon as we were in the air, I put on my headphones and I let my emotions bleed out through the song du jour, as I stared off into the clouds. I nodded my head until I dozed off.

Chapter 2

Olivia

I sat there staring at the phone. I wanted to call my mom and apologize for the way I left, but I wondered if she would even take my call. A part of me wanted to tell her about my life so far while I was out here. I still have no idea of what I want to do with my life, but at least I was managing with a sense of pride. I didn't come out here and lose my mind like she accused me of. She said I was going to come out here, go wild, and end up pregnant with nowhere to go. It's my personal mission not to have the "oh crap I'm pregnant" conversation. I want my husband to want it just as much as I do. The things she said hurt me, but I missed hearing her voice; my brother said she asks about me. He's offered her my number but she doesn't want it. So I know she's still mad at me.

She didn't think it was a good idea for me to come all the way out here with Julia. She wanted me to stay close to home and get my life going there. How could I do that with Montell looming around out there? My mom would die fifty million deaths if she knew about him. There was no way she would've ever approved of me dating him. If I were my friend, I wouldn't have approved of me dating him either. Normally I'm against thugs, I mean what can they really do for you? Curse you out, cheat on you, knock you up, have you put money on their books while they're locked up. That wasn't how Montell and I started out though. In the end, we were your stereotypical ghetto fabulous couple of kids. He cheated, he had baby mommas, we fussed, and we fought, bang bang, shoot 'em up. You know pretty standard stuff. I got tired of the back and forth; it was always the same thing. Some girl telling me she's having my man's baby. Me confronting him about it, him lying saying he don't even know the girl. When the third baby came out looking just like the other two I had enough. I was tired of listening to myself cry about him. I don't care how much his family and I got along and how much they wanted me to be their cousin, daughter in-law, sister in-law, the whole bit, I couldn't do it anymore.

I thought I had a yeast infection, so I went to the doctor, turns out I had chlamydia. The room spun, Montell burned me. As I left the hospital with my prescription, I saw the ghetto fantastic

13

crew, leaving the hospital with Montell's latest rumored sidepiece. I needed to look at the baby. Everyone stopped talking and sort of looked at me as I approached them. I sucked up air, and then I asked to see the baby. She happily showed me her little prince, and sure enough just like the other two he looked just like his father. I told her that her baby was cute, and then I called Julia crying as soon as I got home. She repeated what the doctor said about taking all of my medicine until it was finished. That's when Julia and I kicked up our plan into full gear for me to move out there. Montell wanted to set me up in a place and all this nonsense, but I knew I could never do it. That would've meant coming clean with my mom about him and the lifestyle that I led that neither she nor my little brother had a clue about. The dragon lady would've come out for sure. Running away was a lot easier, even though the dragon lady made sure she sent me off properly.

My mom has been dating her soon to be husband number five for the last four going on five years. The longest she's ever dated before jumping in. I guess because their courtship has gone on so long that's how she's stayed distracted enough for me to be with Montell. My little brother was always with them, and since she was in such a hurry to be with him she never slowed down long enough to verify any of my excuses for why I couldn't go places with them. I didn't have brilliant lies; sometimes I would simply say I didn't want to go. I knew especially on the weekends that when she left she wouldn't be back until late or the next day. Quite a few times Montell has spent the night at my house and she never had a clue. She seemed to only focus on the fact that I wasn't out running the streets.

When I told my mom I wanted to leave, she took it personal and our argument exploded from there. At first, we were arguing about me leaving, and then it turned into everything. She accused me of being selfish and just like my father. That really hurt cause I don't consider myself anything like him.

My father is selfish and he's a jerk. He's extremely blunt and to the point. He would always tell me he couldn't wait until I was eighteen and he didn't have to pay child support anymore. His family made no real effort to know me or interact with me. That's probably why, no, I know it's why I gravitated towards Montell's family. His mom loved me so much, but she enabled him to be who he is. She knew he was selling, and she didn't exactly care until it brought her problems. I guess I can't exactly fault her for embracing her grandchildren it's not like it was their fault either.

I hated when I'd be with them and then one of the baby momma's would come by or bring their babies over. It was so obvious that she had relationships with these girls. She didn't make excuses for Montell, but she would just say stuff like "*what are you going to do?*" She'd shrug it off and keep it going. I guess cause in her world; baby momma's is just something that happened. Montell's father died when he was little, and he got like five or six brothers and sisters all by different mother's too. Child support was enough of a wakeup call for my father not to spread his seed all over the place. Not that he's hurting for money, but he hates parting with his money no matter how big or small the amount is. Mr. Evans still jumps from bed to bed though. My mom's been looking for love this whole time. She finds these losers, thinks she's in love, marries them and then not too long later she's filing for divorce cause the lust that she mistook for love has faded and the guy she's looking at isn't the one. I really think she loved my brother's father. He isn't even one of her previous four husbands. She was so used to being done in, that she didn't even realize that she had adopted some of the same behavior. Royal loved her and she did him wrong, Royal comes around for his son and he's always nice to me, and he even tried to protect me. However, he doesn't want anything to do with my mom. Whenever he has to see my mom his face turns cold and it's downright uncomfortable. I thought they were broken up when her friend Patrick started sniffing around. He'd come over and spend the night and then disappear.

Royal came over late one night unannounced, which was odd cause, he always called or came early. I opened the door and let him in. I knew Patrick was in the room with my mom. Something inside told me not to answer the door when I saw Royal there. It was raining and Royal was excited about something. He said hello to me and chatted with me for a minute. Then he happily walked towards the bedroom. I remember my mom's scream and then I saw Royal beating the mess out of Patrick who was naked. That was the first time I ever saw a man cry. Royal was so hurt and mad! When my mom started screaming at me for letting him in, he protected me and told her that if she laid one finger on me he would do exactly the same to her. The look on his face said he wasn't kidding. My mom tried for a while to get Royal back, but he couldn't stomach her. Now that I'm older, I wonder if he was coming to propose that night. A little while after him, she got married and divorced, now she's with this guy she sees now. I think she's scared of herself a little. She ruined Royal's life, broke his heart. I don't think she trust herself.

I picked up the phone and dialed my mom's number. My little brother answered; as usual, he was happy to hear from me. He told me he missed me and he asked when I was going to come home. I told him I didn't know, but he would be the first person to know as soon as I figured it out. I heard myself ask to speak to our mother, and it was quiet for maybe two minutes before my mom said a stern hello. I started talking immediately; I built up to this very long-winded apology. She didn't say a word; she let me go on and on. I didn't stop talking until the dryness of my mouth forced me to take a drink. My mom was quiet for a minute as she waited for me to continue. Then said a simple, "*fine*." Her way of saying, she forgave me. She asked me a few questions about Georgia and like that…. our feud was over. I was happy she wasn't in an argumentative mood where everything could've spiraled into questions about the whys of it all.

****

"So, Olivia. About your hair?" I reached up to touch the ends of my short tresses. "I thought the short hair was just a phase?"

"There's something wrong with my hair?" I looked in the mirror.

"I honestly thought the short hair was your way of rebelling. Are you going to continue to wear your hair short forever?"

"Until I feel like doing otherwise. I like my hair short. I feel grown with my hair short like this." All of my childhood I wore my hair long. Complete strangers would stop us and tell my mom how pretty my long ponytails were when I was little. When I went to junior high school, I started wearing it down. And in high school I cut it a little. One day Montell's cousin asked me if I ever thought about cutting my hair. I was complaining about how much work it was to take care of it. The thought horrified me at first. As we talked, more like she talked me into it, the more I opened up to the idea. Next thing I know I'm in Montell's bathroom watching my hair fall. When I looked in the mirror initially, it was that feeling like "*oh shoot! What did I do to my hair?*" Then a second a later I felt free. His cousin, who was an inspiring hair stylist, did a wonderful job cutting my hair. My mom screamed and asked me why I did it. I told her it was only hair, and that when I got tired of short hair I would grow it back. Then I kept cutting it and cutting it until I got down to the extremely short curls that I wear today. My hair is about an inch long and I love it this short. Julia on the other hand has finally gotten the hang of handling her hair and she's on am mission to grow her hair out long.

"I understand, but this isn't California. I think your short hair may have something to do with why it's so hard for you to find a part time job. I think you should consider letting it grow out some for now."

"Something as ridiculous as the length of my hair could affect me getting a job flipping burgers?"

"I'm telling you what I see. Give it a try and see for yourself." She said as she walked to the hall closet. Now I felt self-conscious. "You ready?"

Now I didn't want to go, but I had to go. However, Julia was so excited about setting up this double date I didn't have a choice. Her new friend has been nice enough. When school started, the options of available men seemed to rip open. All these students from all over the country seemed to pour in and the harvest was ripe for picking. We caught the bus to the movie theater where we met Julia's friend and his buddy that he brought along. Now that I felt self-conscious about it, I noticed how both of their eyes went to my hair first. Thank goodness, we were going to see a movie, we'd be in the dark for the next two hours.

Ahjani

"Lubbock! I'd like you to meet Thing 1 and Thing 2!" My teammate said as he shook his head at these very pretty girls. "Which one you want?"

"Ooh! I like my men tall and lanky! Pick me!" Thing 1 said as she pressed her soft body up against mine.

"I could make you a sandwich afterwards, I feed the mind, body, and soul." Thing 2 said.

"Oh so it's like that? Thing 1 and Thing 2 gonna ditch a brotha as soon as our star rookie is available?"

"Depends, does Lubbock think he can handle 1 and 2 at once?"

"Yeah, we've heard about you. They call you the energizer bunny cause you keep going and going. I think it would take the both of us just to satisfy you. We could tag team you." Thing 1 said.

"I like the sound of that." Thing 2 said.

I looked at my teammate, he didn't care. "Fine. I'll go back to the lobby and find something else to get into." He smiled and then he walked away.

"What were you doing?" Thing 1 said pushing me backwards into my room.

"Studying." Cause I was. Ever since I've stepped foot on this campus my cup has runneth over with groupies who are perfectly ok with being just another conquest. I'll admit the first month or two it was exciting, I never had this much sex in high school. Now it's that empty desire to fill a need. Thing 1 and Thing 2, they didn't even offer their names. A lot of the time, it's just the idea of sleeping with the star athlete that gets these girls going. None of these girls offer companionship, they open their legs, try to turn me out. Realize they can't hang and then they disappear.

"Well! It's time for a study break." Thing 2 said taking off her coat where she was only wearing nice underwear underneath.

"Right, then you can go back to your studies or relax, the choice is yours." Thing 1 said as she kissed on my neck removing her coat to reveal identical attire.

No foreplay required, I grabbed a condom out of my nightstand. They decided to work together to get me off. I was just starting and they couldn't hang. I finished enough to satisfy me to finish my homework. I thanked the girls for the exercise and then I told them I had to get back to my studies. "You're even better than the rumors. I'm determined to conquer you. I wasn't prepared."

"Right me neither. We'll be back."

I went back to my studies, and then I looked at the clock. It was almost seven. I picked up the phone, "hello?"

"Princess Fiona! I need you!" She laughed, "Thing 1 and Thing 2 interrupted my studies. I need to burn off this energy."

"Do I get you for the night?"

"It looks that way. It's getting late."

Her voice smiled, "great! Let me get ready, maybe we can get a bite to eat before the festivities?"

"Sounds good to me." I showered then I waited. Fiona is my "buddy"; she's the closest thing I've got to a girlfriend out here. She's a complete feminist, and she goes on and on about women's rights and equality, which is how I believe our arrangement, began. Women can have sex just like men was the argument. What she didn't understand is that I was making the case that men need to feel loved just like women do. However, my point went over her head. I guess to prove her point that women could get down just like men she decided that we would have sex that night. I wasn't hanging with her for sex. I didn't even look at Fiona that way anymo, initially I was interested. I like an intelligent and independent woman, that's what I grew up around. However, Fiona told me I would never be anything more to her than a brother type. She quickly changed her tune from brother to buddy as I hit it the first time. So far, she's the only girl out here who could hang with me sexually, but she makes sure that I understand that we only have sex and that I shouldn't read more into the act than what it is. Although I know I'm the only person she spreads her legs for, she's drilled it in. This is just sex.

We were debating as usual, I could say the sky is blue and just to argue with me and prove that she has a valid point she will argue that it's more cerulean. A girl walked up to our table and they did the "*hey it's been so long since I've seen you*" dance. Fiona introduced me to Julia who said she was on a double date with her good friend. Fiona told them to join us at the long counter where we sat eating our pizza slices. Julia introduced us to her date, his friend, and her friend. I said a polite hello. Introduced myself and then listened as Fiona brought them in on our current argument. That's when the battle of the sexes began. None of us were saying that it was ok that women made less doing the same job as men. However, none of us would agree to take a pay cut to stand up for women's rights. Sometimes Fiona argues just to have an argument. As it got late, as we were all lost in our conversation, the guys had to literally run back to their dorm before they missed curfew. Fiona told Julia and her friend that we would take them home. "So Fiona is this your boyfriend?" Julia asked her like I wasn't sitting there.

"NO! I don't have time or patience for a boyfriend. Ahjani and I are friends, buddies if you will." Fiona acted like the question was ridiculous.

"Open relationship?"

"If you could call what we have a relationship."

"Wait a minute! So Fiona are you trying to say I'm nobody?" I was getting irritated. I hate when she tries to act like she doesn't care.

"I'm saying we're just friends. I have no claim to you and you to me. You are free to do whatever you want, you know that." Then she looked at Julia, "you interested?"

Julia looked me up and down, "if I thought athletes were capable of genuine love I would be."

"So you believe the stereotypes? Athletes can't have monogamous relationships?"

"You all travel, and then when you're home I know the local groupies keep you all pretty busy."

"Athletes need love too."

"Yes, but you look for love in all the wrong places." She smiled.

"Sometimes when I'm alone in my room and I stare at the walls and in the back of my mind I hear my conscience call. Telling me I need a girl who's as sweet as a dove, for the first time in my life, I see I need love."

We laughed then we got in the car, Julia kept smiling at me and watching everything I did. Originally I would think she was offering more, but her constant direction back to the game, my stats, and things like that let me know she was a glorified groupie, a gold digger looking to hook her million dollar hopeful. "What kind of girl do you like?" Julia asked

"Initially I liked Fiona, then she spoke." I laughed.

"Forget you Ahjani! Pardon me for having a brain!" She laughed.

"So you are attracted to her physically?"

"Yeah, she's alright. Why do you ask?"

"I'm trying to pinpoint what kind of girl you like. Do you like light skinned or dark skinned, short or tall, curvy or athletic types." She looked at her friend, "long hair, or short hair?"

"I don't have a color preference, I love the rainbow. I definitely like curvy women; I'm from Richmond California. Curvy women are the norm."

"I'm from Castro Valley California!" Her friend happily interjected.

"Castro Valley is close enough to the Bay for you to claim the Bay as your home. You better declare it from now on."

"Get back on track, go on." Julia interrupted, "long hair or short hair."

"I prefer long hair."

Julia smiled, "ok so why would you be interested in Fiona? Miss lighter skinned, long hair athletic physique over here."

"I guess her hair caught my attention first. It wasn't deep, it was like oh she's cute. She speaks, then the attraction subsided."

"Forget you!" Fiona laughed

"You two ever sleep together?"

"Um, Olivia? Does she ever get in your business like this?" Fiona asked.

"Completely!"

"All you need to know is that Ahjani and I aren't together. If you wanna sleep with him, take a number and get in line. You don't need to concern yourself with what Ahjani and I do."

"I'll pass. I'm not looking for just a buddy."

"Your loss, Ahjani's an excellent buddy to have." Fiona flicked my chin.

"I feel like I'm being shown off at a slave auction."

"It's ok Mandingo! As soon as we drop them off I'll make it up to you." Fiona teased.

We dropped her friends off and then Fiona reached between my legs and started massaging me. She asked me what I thought of Julia. I told her I didn't think anything of Julia as I leaned my head back on my headrest enjoying her touch. She asked me if I was mad at her, the tell tell sign that her desire was coming forth. Fiona could talk the talk, but when it came to it, she was all female. The shock and pleasure that spreads over her face the first time I make her cum is always the same. Each time it's like she can't believe that I am able to tap that nerve. By the time I finish with her, she's speechless and in need of cuddles. We normally pretend for the night, and as soon as I leave it's back to the same ole same.

Olivia

"He's not the only guy to feel like that. People in general feel like that." Julia said undressing.

"Fine, I'll let my hair grow out long enough to braid it. Long hair is such a chore."

"You were awfully quiet tonight." She smiled

"I was listening," I said hoping she would let it go.

"I saw how you looked at him. You liked him didn't you." She gave me a knowing look.

"He probably thinks you like him with all your questions."

She shrugged, "maybe I do too. But I know you like him is my point."

"Doesn't matter, he didn't look in my direction once."

"Cause you were sitting over there tight lipped, jacket zipped all the way up and short hair. You could have him if you want him. But you're going to have to let your hair grow out."

"Shouldn't I want a man who wants me for who I am?"

"Please Olivia this short hair is not you. I thought you said you're over Montell?"

"I am!"

"Then let the short hair go. The only thing you had control over in that relationship was the length of your hair. You didn't even get to say when you got some from him. You had no power. Now that that's over, use your powers for good." She smiled big, "they call Ahjani the energizer rabbit. He keeps going and going." Julia closed her eyes and shook, "can you even imagine what that's like?"

"Sounds painful."

"Oh, like thug loving isn't? I think you could handle it."

"If you like him why are you encouraging me to go after him?"

"Girl please! I don't have time to start over. Oscar and I are almost to date five, I don't want to start over, and momma needs to get her a taste. Besides, you need a man and fast, you moan in your sleep. I know you're pent up."

I laughed, and then I looked in the mirror. Maybe she did have a point about my hair. "Do you know a good braider?"

"Of course I do, I'll give you Peaches' number in the morning."

Ahjani

"AHJANI!" She gasped for air, "YOU'RE TRYING TO KILL ME!"

"Oh yeah! Who's just a buddy now?" I said as I stroked her deeper.

Fiona's eyes rolled back in her head as she succumbed to my knowledge of her body. She was begging me to take it easy on her, but I refused. She ran her mouth all night about how I was just a buddy, offered me to her friend as if she could handle it. I don't like feeling like I don't matter; it was time to punish her. Every time she falls asleep, I let her nap then I take her again. Fiona's mouth can only get my name out before she's surrendering to my stroke. "Are you mad at me?" She panted.
I went deeper and she screamed. After the last round, she called herself coming out here to the couch to avoid me; this couch was the no sex zone. No matter how hot and heavy we got sitting on this couch, she wouldn't do it. She cried out to God to save her. "Stop pretending like you don't like me Princess Fiona." I growled in her ear.

"You're too...... OH GOD! OH GOD! OH GOD!" She screamed as she tightened around me signaling another release.

This one was so big that it forced me to release with her. I went to the bathroom, flushed the condom holding my soldiers captive, and then I walked back to the bed feeling good about myself. When Fiona got back in the bed, she collapsed on me. "You're welcome!" I kissed her forehead.

"I like you Ahjani," her voice was low. "I'm not stupid, all those girls throwing their selves at you. Stop trying to blow my cover."

"Stop acting like anyone can have me. Your friend Julia is a gold digger, I'm not interested."

"Doesn't mean you wouldn't sleep with her." She had a point, when I didn't respond she turned her back to me and went back to sleep.

Chapter 3

Olivia

"Welcome to Spunkmeyer's how may I help you today?" I asked my regulars.

"I want bubblegum!" The oldest girl said.

"I want peppermint please." The littlest little girl said.

"Good job! Manners are always important." Their father told them, and then he looked at me with a smile. "I'll have the usual." This family comes in at least two times a week for after school ice cream. Sometimes the wife comes and when she does, the husband is still nice, but when she's not here, he flirts. I scoop their ice cream and take their payment with a smile, after all their repeated business keeps me employed. "How long does it take to get your hair like that?"

"All day," I tried to maintain my smile as he admired my braids.

"Black hair on cinnamon skin is very alluring." His eyes pleaded for a signal that I was open to his advances.

"Thanks," then I called out to the girls who were enjoying their cones at the table. "is your mommy coming today?"

"No, she's working."

"Tell her I said hi," then I continued on with my behind the counter task. I don't know what he thinks this is.
Then a group of guys walked in the door loud and laughing. "Welcome to Spunkmeyer's how may I help you today?"

"Well obviously we've come for ice cream!" One guy said being a smart aleck.

Days like this are annoying enough. I forgot to refill my prescription for my birth control so my period decided to come in full force today now that I'm on week two of this nonsense. Last thing I want to do is to be bending over these cold freezers scooping ice cream for smart alecks and men who are looking for affairs. Still I put on my best smile and do my job. "Let me know when you're ready."

All of them were tall, and wearing sweats like they were a uniform. One of the guys steps out from the back. "So say I want a HUGE sundae, how huge can you make it?"

I recognized him, it was Ahjani. Sadly, he didn't seem to recognize me. "We have a five scoop sundae, that's as big as I can make it." I watched his eyes as he looked around the menu and then into the freezers.

"That sounds good, now to decide whether I want potassium or my brownie fix? Decisions, decisions. Y'all know what you want?" He asked his teammates, "somebody has to go before me while I try to decide."

As I scooped for one of his team mates, a couple of girls walked in. They got all giggly as they introduced their selves to the team, mostly looking at Ahjani. The rest of the team looked at these girls as if they were too common for their liking, and they were used to girls throwing their selves at their feet. Ahjani was the only nice one to pose for a picture and let them down nicely. One by one, I helped the teammates as I watched Ahjani now charm my little regulars as he talked to their family. When it was Ahjani's turn, he came back apologizing for not making up his mind yet. I asked him if he was against bananas and brownies together, and he said no. I asked him for his flavor choices and then I told him I would create his sundae. He told me and then more females walked in the ice cream parlor, I swear this many girls never come in here. I happily interrupted Ahjani's conversation as I told him to meet me at the register. He looked at me, "do you go to my school? You look familiar?"

"I'm Julia's friend."

"Julia?" He was jogging his brain to remember.

Obviously, she didn't leave any lasting marks on him thank goodness. "You were with your buddy. We had pizza, you guys gave us a ride back to our place."

"Oh right, you're from the Bay right? What's your name again?"

"Olivia."

"Olive Oil, nice to meet you again. This looks delicious." Then he took a spoonful of his sundae.

"Olive Oil?" I liked my new name.

"Yep, that's my name for you. You changed your hair didn't you?"

I touched my braids, "yea. I'm growing it out."

"That's good I like long hair on women. If those braids are any indication you're going to be a complete knock out with long hair."

Oh my God! Oh my God! Is he flirting with me? "Well if I knew all I had to do was grow my hair out so you'd notice me I never would've cut it."

He smiled as he took another spoonful of his sundae into his mouth. "You hooked a brotha up I see." He smiled as he spoke lowly.

I put my finger up to my mouth as I tried to speak seductively. "I'll only do that for you."

He smiled wider, "what else would you do for me?"

"I don't want your friend to get mad at me."

"My friend? Oh, you mean Princess Fiona? Her royal highness has made a love connection, she barely has time for me anymore."

"Oh that's too bad. Does that mean you're looking for a new friend?"

"I could be. Are you that somebody? I could be looking for you. Are you a good girl or a vixen?"

"Why couldn't I be both?"

He smiled, "stop playing with me. When you wanna go out?"

Suddenly I remembered this curse of a period that would not subside until next week as my body readjusted to the hormones. "What's your schedule like next week?"

His smile dropped, "you gonna make me wait all the way until next week? You got your period or something?"

His boldness caught me off guard and I started laughing an embarrassed laugh. "What?"

"Maybe I just want a chance to get to know the pretty girl. I promise not to turn you out on the first date."

"How do you know there would be more than one date?"

"No one who makes a sundae like this could have only one date with me. You're a guaranteed three date minimum."

I smiled, "what about tomorrow night?"

"I've got a game. How about you come to my game and then we can go out after."

"You don't live in a dorm? Won't you break curfew?"

"I could sleep on the steps of my dorm for the first time ever. I'll see if one of my teammates can sneak me in. Do we have a date?"

"Ok."

"I'm not going to get your number so you can't fake on me. I'll leave a ticket for you Olive Oil, see you at my game." He walked away eating his sundae.

Ahjani

I spotted her in the stands watching me. Little Ms. Olive Oil was dressed nicely in grey and blue. She pulled her braids up into a ponytail. After the game, she came down to the floor. I thanked her for showing up. I introduced her to a few of the basketball wives as we called them, and I asked them to show her where to meet us. In the locker room, a lot of my teammates gave me props for my choice. Truth is, I'm tired of groupies. I liked the feeling before and I wanted it back. I liked having a specific girlfriend at my games cheering me on. I need to make love in the worst way. All this random sex is OLD! So I decided to stop playing the game. Little Ms. Olive Oil happened to pop up right as I made this decision. So far, she's proven to be promising. I got showered and dressed then I met Olive Oil in front of the locker room. I gave her a hug, she smelled like soap, but she wasn't wearing any perfume. I love perfume on women, soap is good too.

"Where are you two going to eat?" Spencer asked me.

"We hadn't decided, what you feel like eating?" I asked Olive.

"I'm not picky, it doesn't matter."

"Good! Come out with my lady and me. We need to celebrate our win together anyways Lubbock."

"As long as that's ok with Olive." I looked at her.

She smiled, "that's fine."

"Courtney," he called out to his woman. "We're doubling with Lubbock and his girl."

Courtney smiled then she ended her conversation and walked over. She introduced herself to us. Up close, she didn't look like a student. I haven't ever been this close to her before, but then again I didn't care. If Spencer likes it, I love it. I put my arm around Olive as we walked to Courtney's car. As we pulled up to the restaurant Spencer announced that he was paying and we needed to order up, sky was the limit. Little Miss Olive Oil waited to see what I ordered before she made a decision. I liked that she was paying attention. Spencer ordered six different kinds of sushi rolls, and then he told me to do the same. Olive ordered three and Courtney ordered a couple different Saki's for our table. When Olive started to relax, Courtney started in with her questions. She asked her what school she went to, how we met, what our long term plans were. I told Courtney this was our first date and to pump the brakes after Olive answered some of the questions I would've asked her myself. "Oh Spencer! They haven't even done it yet." She said like she was reminiscing. Clearly, she could not hold her weight against the powers of her Saki. "Remember our first time?" She smiled.

Spencer smiled at her, "yes I do." He looked at me, "that's how she got me." He winked as he bumped me.

"Gurl! He had a girlfriend and everything. I didn't let that stop me, what Courtney wants, Courtney gets!"

"And you got me baby!"

"And I'm never letting go! You can have me anyway you want me." She announced.

"I've had you in every way possible."

"That's why I got him, he's not going anywhere!" She smiled. "Gurl! These groupies will do anything to take your man. You gotta hold him down with both hands and any orifice you can."

I spit out my Saki, "Graphic mental! Cut it out! I don't want to hear all that!"

Olive looked at Courtney, she was not amused. "I'm all for keeping my man happy, but not at the expense of ruining myself. I'm not into butt plugs or any backdoor experimenting. He's not even your husband, not that I would do it then either. But you let him wear you out every which way possible and then it doesn't work out. What do you have left?"

"Little girl please, if you don't do it. Some other female will. And she'll be calling your man daddy and begging for more."

"Then let him wear her out, I refuse!"

I leaned over and spoke in her ear. "Just so you know outside of an occasional lick, grab, cushion for my lap I'm not an explorer of the unknown. These fools are crazy! Let's play nice cause this bill has got to be over three hundred or more, and then we'll escape. Deal?"

"Deal," she exhaled in relief.

"Oh and the Saki has me a little twisted, so please grant me a pardon as my hand can no longer resist making contact with your firm and supple assets in five, four, three, two, one." Then I rubbed her butt.

Olive laughed, "pardon granted this time."

Olivia

I got out of bed with a smile on my face. I hummed as I went in the closet to get my clothes for the day. I was trying to be quiet, but I was too happy. When I stepped out of the closet, Julia had her pillow over her head. "Sorry!" I said tiptoeing.

"Don't apologize now, I'm up. Did you do it yet?"

She always asks me that every time I come home from a date. I know she just wants to know if the rumors are true. With as much as I'm starting to like Ahjani, I don't know if I could bring myself to tell her if it's all true. I don't want her looking at him like that. The more time that passes the more I'm seeing, and sometimes I wonder how I missed little things about her personality. I don't remember her being competitive, self-centered. She's still nice and she still looks out for me. But she's all in my business for real. "Not yet, he says he can wait for me."

"What are you waiting for? He's probably still doing Fiona while he waits for you."

"She has a boyfriend."

"Is that supposed to mean something? Who respects relationships anymore?"

"I gotta go get in the shower, I'm gonna be late."

"You two still going to do the photo-shoot this afternoon?"

"Yes, we'll be at the park at 3pm sharp." Then I closed the bedroom door and got in the shower. After my morning classes, I met Ahjani at the bus stop. He was dressed nicely in a sweater, pea coat, boots, and jeans. "You look delicious!"

"Thank you," he said coming in for a kiss. "Likewise." When we got to the apartment, I took off my jacket and then we kissed again. "You're wearing the perfume I bought you." Then he kissed me deeper.

"I like the way it smells on me. It's not too strong. How did you ever find it?"

"I got a good nose I guess." He had longing in his eyes as he looked down at me.

I knew Julia was with her mentor and she wouldn't be home until after the shoot. We had the place and the bed to ourselves. Julia and I shared a bed, and I didn't want to do it for the first time on the couch, so I guess I was waiting for this opportunity. "Can you help me decide which dress to wear?" Ahjani shook his head yes. I sat him on the bed. I opened the closet and then I brought out both of my dresses. A brown dress and a grey dress. "Which one do you like?"

"Both of them are nice, but I think we need you to bring some color to our picture. We've got a wonderful fall backdrop; my clothes are kind of monotones. What color splash do you have to offer?"

I tried to pull back my irritation cause I just knew he'd pick the grey dress. I looked in my closet and most of my clothes were monotone, muted in color. I brought out a burgundy dress that was almost fuchsia. "What about this one?"

"Perfect!" He said looking at the dress. "Come here, what time we got to be at the park?"

"3," I said getting a little nervous. Was this really about to happen?

He looked at the clock next to the bed, "it's not even twelve yet. Can I have you before we go?"

"Have me?" I hung my dress on the closet door then I stood in front of him.

"Yes," he watched my eyes as he unbuttoned my shirt. "Wouldn't you say now is the time?" He buried his head in my breast sucking and kissing on them. "You smell so good."

I rubbed his head, "I didn't say yes."

Ahjani abruptly stopped kissing me and he put his hands up like he was surrendering. "You don't want me to touch you?"

I started laughing, "I do. I was just saying that I hadn't said yes."

"So are you saying yes now?" He said as his hands went under my skirt pushing it up. "I've been a good boy, it's been just me and my hand since we started dating. No hoes, I've been waiting for you."

"Not even Fiona?" I smiled.

"Not even the princess herself and you know her highness was not happy. I've been waiting for you." He started massaging me.

"Why?"

"I'm tired of having sex, I want to make love."

I moaned cause his touch felt so good. "That would imply that you love me."

He stood up and unbuttoned my skirt to move it out of the way. He looked at my body, "I love you Olivia Paisley Evans."

I was so happy I waited and didn't say it first. Hearing his declaration of love made everything in me come alive. We undressed each other like we were unwrapping presents. He put a condom on the pillow next to my head as he laid me down. I watched Ahjani put his condom on; I couldn't help but notice that Montell the only man I've known until now was bigger.

When Ahjani slowly entered me, I realized that he was still big enough for everything I needed. He watched me to make sure he wasn't hurting me and he asked me if I was ok. I politely climaxed and it was ok, but in my mind, I was thinking about how rumors always make things out to be bigger than they really are. He watched me for a minute, and then he asked me if I was ok. When I said yes, he asked if I would like to keep going. Of course, I said yes.

He turned me on my side and he cuddled me from behind, as he kept moving. I could see the tree outside our window, the birds on their perch looked like they were telling him to work me over. Ahjani got up and raised my leg while he rubbed me. Air escaped me as I climaxed harder this time. I thought he would be spent as he nutted. He got up went to the bathroom, I heard him flush. And then he came back with another condom in hand. I looked at him in disbelief. He asked me if I was ready, I looked at him with wide eyes as I said yes.

He flipped me over and put my butt in the air as he slapped my butt and put his condom on. He slapped my butt like it was his percussion instrument. Each stroke hit my throat, so much for thinking he was lacking. Maybe it was the position but I couldn't move, all I could do was feel, and Ahjani felt glorious! "Cum for me baby! Let daddy hear you purr one more time for me!" He flipped me again, drug my body to the edge of the bed pushed my legs all the way back and went in. This can't be real! He definitely was pent up. He nutted again, went to the bathroom. I did a double take as he came out still hard. I asked him what drug he was on. He said he was high on me as he grabbed another condom.

This time sound escaped me as I came so hard I told him not to touch me, but he said "Daddy's ready now." Ready for what my mind screamed. He stood and put my butt back up in the air. I gripped the sheets as he worked me. Then he made me sit up in his lap as he bent his knees to support us. I had no idea he was this strong. He held us up for a while then he turned sat down spread my legs as he rubbed me some more. "Daddy thinks this kitty has one more good purr left in her. Purr for daddy!"

At his command, my body tightened around him and we blew together. Ahjani fell backwards on the bed catching his breath. I slowly got up making sure I didn't take the condom with me. He slowly got up this time and went to the bathroom. I climbed under the covers and then I watched the door. Ahjani apparently has no problem with me seeing him naked. Montell always kept his shirt on at the very least. And he was always quick to cover up when we were done. Ahjani got on the bed and he pulled the covers off of me. He kissed my stomach, my chest, and then my mouth. "I think we properly broke that kitty in what you think?"

"That was amazing!"

He smiled, "on a scale of one to five, five being the highest. What's my score?"

"Are you kidding? That was ten platinum stars, have you always had sex like that?"

"It's a learned talent of course but wait until I give you the good stuff." He raised his eyebrows.

I sat up on my elbows. "You mean to tell me it gets better than that?"

He kissed me, "a whole lot better."

My brain swished at the thought of it. "I don't know if I can hang Ahjani." I was now scared.

"You'll get there, you'll be calling me daddy, and begging for catnip."

"You're so sure?"

"It's guaranteed," he smiled.

We talked, we showered, and we changed the bedding that was covered in wet spots. When we got to the photo-shoot at 2:50pm, I tried to act as normal as possible. Julia still whispered in my ear as we took our positions, "you're walking funny."

Ahjani

"Ooh! I like this." Olive said admiring a dress on the rack.

"I like that one better." I said pointing at the pink one.

"Do you have a hidden obsession with pink or something? Every time you pick something out for me it's pink."

"My momma said girls wear pink and boys wear blue. I like ladies in pink."

She stared at me, "does your momma wear pink all of the time?"

"That's not even funny. No, she does not. If it wasn't a good color on you I wouldn't choose it."

Olive held the dress up to herself in the mirror. "It does look good on me doesn't it."

I put my arms around her, and then I bit her neck. "Downright sexy. Buy the dress and then I want you to try it on for me when we get home."

"What if Julia has company?"

"Then that means the living room is all ours. Either way I'm going in." I smiled at her in the mirror.

Olive's eyes got that dreamy look and then she said she was buying the dress. I smacked her butt and told her that was my good girl. "You wanna split a cinnabun?" She asked as she paid for her dress.

"Can't today."

She shook her head, "one of these days I'm going to need you to write down the eating schedule. Complex carbs days, protein days, it's too confusing."

"You're coming along just fine, you'll get the hang of it." The cashier kept trying to make eye contact with me whenever Olivia wasn't looking. I looked everywhere but at her.

In the food court, I watched Olive eat her cinnabun with so much appreciation. I couldn't wait to get her home. "Well hello everyone, imagine running into my buddy after all these months without so much as a returned phone call. I thought you might've dropped out of school. When do you ever not call me back?"

"Oh Princess Fiona you know I've been drinking love nectar from the fountains of Olive Oil." I smiled, Olive didn't.

Fiona laughed hard, "I don't know where you come up with all this stuff."

"I've been blessed with a wonderful imagination. How have you been?"

"Missing you, I'm single." She said blatantly.

"I'm sorry to hear that. I'm in love with this woman, I haven't much time for anyone else." I kissed Olive's hand as she smiled.

Fiona looked shocked, surprised, and hurt. She finally looked at my Olive. "I didn't realize you two were in love. I'm happy for you two." She tried to sound happy for us.

"Thank you."

Then Fiona walked away, I guess she didn't believe me when I said I was looking for love. I guess I'm supposed to play the field forever.

When we got to Olive's place Julia was cooking up a storm. She said her man was coming for dinner. Olive only heard she wouldn't be in the room. She took my hand and said she'd clean the kitchen when Julia was done. Olive put the dress on, turned to look at herself in the mirror, and I went in. Little Miss Olive Oil was trying her hardest to be quiet; my catnip had her kitty purring so loud there was no way to hold it back. When I went to the bathroom to flush my condom, Julia and her man were on the couch. She was riding him and he was so lost in the sauce that he didn't notice her staring at me. She licked her lips at me and worked him harder, which made him cry out. Julia was topless and not bad looking at all. She asked me if I liked it, and he replied yes, she asked again as her rhythm picked up. I stood there and crossed my arms. She grabbed the top of his fade as she buried his face in her breast and she asked me if I liked it again. I went back in the room and shut the door. Olive and I were in the middle of our own action. I was now faced with a dilemma, if I put on another condom, I'd have to dispose of it and risk walking back out there on them again. Olive's on the pill and is very diligent about taking it on time every day. I went in, skin to skin. Olive immediately purred, screamed, and proceeded to speak in tongues from this dose of catnip. Without bathroom breaks I had the kitty purring louder than I think she even knew she could reach. We took a nap on top of the covers; we woke to Julia walking in the room stating she needed to get something out of the closet. Olive threw the covers over me as if she could stop her from seeing what she's already seen. Julia told Olive they were waiting for us to eat. Olive put on a loose T-shirt and baggy sweats. I put my shirt and jeans back on. We took the bedding off and then we went to the table. The table was small with only four chairs, one at each section. I sat directly across from Julia, with Olive on my right. Julia's man was on my left.

"My brotha I need a list of every vitamin you take and how you're taking them. You were representing for the mutha land in there." Julia's man said raising his hand to give me five. Olive started rubbing my foot with hers to calm me. I looked at his hand like he had to be kidding me. "My bad, y'all in love or something?"

"As a matter of fact we are." I glared at him, Olive's foot stopped moving.

"Oh! My bad, I'm sorry."

Julia looked at Olive who kept her head down, she looked annoyed. "I'm sorry my best friend didn't tell me either."

"Are you ashamed of me?" I looked at Olive.

"Baby not at all, it's just that you're so high profile. I try to keep a low profile on us."

"Even from me?" Julia looked angry.

"I had no intention of malice. There are just something's that should stay between a man and a woman."

I kissed Olive's hand, "as you see it's no secret with me. If you're not declaring the same love from the highest mountaintop I'm going to take that the wrong way. Understood?"

Olive bowed her head, "yes." Then she said daddy just above a whisper and she looked at me. I smiled and kissed her hand again. "We have a new filter, would you like some water with your meal?"

"Thank you." I said watching Olive get up. When the foot I thought was Olive's started massaging my foot again in the same way. I suddenly lost my appetite and I pushed away from the table.

****

"It's time to watch you get spanked in your own arena!" Omar said overly confident as usual.

35

I smiled, "in your dreams! This is my house!" This fool has always wanted to challenge me since high school. He's lucky that he was dating my cousin back then, and Kendra seemed really happy with him. That's the only thing that ever stopped me from cracking him in the face.

It was always the same thing, when he realized he couldn't beat me he'd start fouling me. I could ALWAYS count on it. My free throws are polished and I swish every time! Omar sat over to the side with the recruiter watching my every move. He needs to choose a school for next year. I really hope he doesn't pick mine. I would love to rub his face in my victory over him.

Omar is actually pretty good, but he's too emotional. At least whenever Kendra was around he'd push it back some. Mister ball of emotions couldn't ever really pull it together. Olive and the rest of the basketball wives were waiting by the locker room for us. Omar was looking as she congratulated me on a game well played. I called him over and I introduced Omar to Olivia. He acted like a normal person as we all talked. He gave me a pound and nod on Olivia. No matter how much he wanted to hate on my situation, he couldn't deny that my girl was top notch.

Fiona approached slowly and interjected herself into our conversation. My Olive shot me a look. Spencer asked if we were coming to celebrate with him and Courtney and I told Omar I'd catch up to him this summer. He told me that he and his momma were going to move wherever he decided to go to school, and I was welcome to come out and visit. I got his number then I told him I would be in touch.

Chapter 4

Olivia

Courtney was so excited, Spencer has an agent and he was going to enter the draft this year. She was telling me about all the plans they had for Spencer after he was drafted. She was so excited cause it was all about to come true. Suddenly the entire arena gasped and we saw Spencer on the ground. Referees were running to him blowing whistles and his teammates were rallying around him to see if he was ok. Spencer was holding his knee and he couldn't get up. Courtney screamed a blood-curdling scream and she ran down to the main floor. Security wouldn't let her pass. They took Spencer out and Ahjani looked at me with worry in his eyes. I ran down to Courtney and I asked them where they were taking Spencer. They told us they were taking him to the hospital. I drove Courtney's car to the hospital while she cried hysterically. The assistant coach that rode in the ambulance with Spencer told us the X-rays showed a tear in his ACL. Courtney cried harder as she ran away. I decided to give her space and find out more information from the coach. He said Spencer was going to need surgery and they had no idea if he'd be able to play again. I sat down devastated as I just remembered when Spencer entered the arena, everyone was screaming his name, and Courtney was blowing him kisses. The rest of the team came as soon as the game was over. They told Spencer they won the game for him. Ahjani asked me where Courtney was. I told him she went outside to probably get some air, but it had been a minute since she went outside. When Ahjani and another player went out, they came back saying they didn't see her. I said she was probably in her car so she could cry privately. A different car was parked where I parked her car. Ahjani shook his head and said it was a cold world. I couldn't believe that she abandoned him like this. She said he was her man, and just a couple of hours ago she was excited telling me about all their plans. When they brought Spencer out he asked where

Courtney was. I didn't know what to say. The coach patted his shoulders and told him he would drive him home. One of Ahjani's teammates drove us back to my place. The whole time he was going off about how much of a gold digger Courtney was and how he couldn't believe she left him like that. Ahjani was quiet and thoughtful. When we walked in the door, I closed the bedroom door cause Julia was in the bed. I put on a pot of hot water to make Ahjani and I some tea. "Are you going to be ok?"

"I can't believe she left him like that. She's good, a real professional. I thought she loved him."

"I did too, up until the moment he hurt himself she was talking about the plans she had for him and his career. She ran like she owed him money."

Ahjani

I looked at Olive, "would you leave me like that?"

"Never!"

"This is the classic story, a gold digger will serve you up good while there's possibly something in it for them. And then as soon as they think they can catch a bigger fish, or they think this well has run dry they switch up. What would it take for you to leave me?"

"If you hit me, there's no negotiating around that, or if you cheated on me."

"That's it? Those are your only conditions? What if I decide that I don't want to go into the NBA? What if I continue to work towards being the poor man's dentist? Would you stand by me in that endeavor?"

"Of course I would. None of that changes who you are and all that you mean to me?"

"Olive, you're not the first girl to tell me you love me in a way that makes me want to believe you. I know she's not you, but one day she disappeared. I know her parents were making it hard for us to be together, but one day she stopped trying. She gave up on me. How much would it take for you to give up on me?"

"I'm not a child Ahjani. There are different rules involved for adults."

"Like?" I watched her eyes looking for a sign that she was lying to me.

"I don't need permission to be with you. It's always been my choice to love you. I'm here, I'm not going anywhere."

I looked at her hair, "when are you going to start wearing your hair?"

She looks surprised that I mentioned her hair, she touched her braids gently. "It's just been easier to manage with my braids."

"I want to run my fingers through your hair. How long is it now?"

"Last time I took my hair down it was at my neck."

"You should start wearing your hair down."

"What does my hair have to do with this conversation?"

"Nothing, I'm nerved up. That was a lot of reality. I love you Olivia and I never want to experience what Spencer is going through."

"Not with me."

****

"I've been trying to find you all of this time. Where did you go?" Nellie said as she cried.

"You stopped fighting for us, I had to move on."

"I had to slow down, I couldn't keep up." Then she pointed to a pink bassinet in the corner. "Ahjani we had a baby."

My heart started pounding as I approached the bassinet. I picked up the baby in disbelief. I was torn between two reactions, I wanted to be overjoyed that Nellie was back. However, I was livid that I wasn't a part of my child's life. I will never be my father! Nellie cried saying that she's always told me how messed up she was and that I never should've gotten involved with her. As I held my little girl and bounced her there was a knock at the door. Nellie opened it and Olivia walked in. She asked me what was going on, and I told her the truth. That I had no idea about the baby until now. Olivia was extremely angry and I didn't understand until she pointed out that she and Nellie were wearing the same outfit. I subconsciously changed everything about Olivia to be just like Nellie. I apologized because I didn't realize I was doing it. When I apologized to Olivia, Nellie got mad and snatched the baby. She started running from me and no matter what I couldn't catch her. Olivia accused me of never really loving her. Nellie was gone and nowhere to be found. I begged Olivia to stay. Olivia woke me up cause I was calling out to her in my sleep. I hugged her and I begged her not to leave me. She held me back as she told me she wasn't going anywhere.

In the morning, I walked Olivia to her class, I held onto her. I ditched my morning class and I called my sister Ahjanae instead. She put my niece Erin on the phone at one point. I was homesick and I needed to see my family. When Ahjanae called our momma on three-way at work, she gave me a hard time about not calling as regularly as I should. I told them that I wanted them to meet my girlfriend. I love the women in my life. They've been excited about meeting Olivia from the first time I mentioned her. My momma told me to call her back with the dates and they'd have our tickets waiting.

Olivia

Ahjani couldn't stop smiling, he's so excited for me to meet his family. I had no idea of what to expect; would they be like Montell's family? Worse? Or better? They sound like good people from the things Ahjani says. As soon as we got in the rental car I wanted to move back home, I miss the Bay. Ahjani pulled into a driveway and a girl came running out. "I miss you Jani! I miss you!" She threw her arms around him and squeezed. Ahjani hugged her then he told me to come over. He introduced me to his little sister Audra. She smiled genuinely at me and then she gave me a hug. She told Ahjani that I was very pretty.

The smell of food hit my nose as soon as we approached the front door.

"Hey baby how you doing?" A lady from across the street called out as she approached with a smile on her face.

Ahjani gave her a big hug as he told her he was doing well and he asked how she was doing. She said she was good. "Olivia this is our neighbor Ms. Lorraine. Ms. Lorraine this is my girlfriend Olivia."

"Oh Ahjani she's so pretty. I know she has to be a good person for you to bring her home, Aquilla don't play when it comes to her babies. It's nice to meet you sweetheart."

"Is D-Rick or D coming by anytime soon?"

"Who knows with them boys. They mostly pop up these

days. When do you leave? I'll tell them you're out here next time I talk to them."

"We leave Saturday."

"That's good, we get to have you a whole week. I gotta run, but I'll see you soon." She hugged us again and then she got in her car and left.

"Hi I'm Ahjanae it's nice to finally meet you. This is my daughter Erin."

"It's nice to finally meet you all in person, I've heard so many wonderful things about you."

Then I knew it was his mom by her voice. She gave me a big hug and happily welcomed me into their home. We sat in the living room, quickly my nervousness subsided and it was like I was talking to my family. I called my mom and I told her we landed and that I'd see her tomorrow. When I talked to my little brother he whispered that his father wanted me to call him.

When I talked to Royal he asked me if he was going to have an opportunity to meet the young man I was bringing home. I broke down; I could tell my tears startled him. I always loved him, I wasn't sure that he loved me. Royal couldn't understand anything I was saying cause I was crying so hard. Ahjani took the phone and spoke with Royal for a while then I realized that Royal was giving Ahjani directions to his house in Hayward. Ahjanae had Erin in the tub, and his mom would need to go to bed soon for work the next day. Audra happily volunteered herself to come with us. During the car ride over, Ahjani asked Audra to sing for us. I had to turn around and look at her. Her voice is amazing. She said she's more interested in acting then singing. She said her music teacher is encouraging her to look into Broadway plays and shows.

Royal opened his door with the biggest smile on his face.

He gave me a huge hug. "Look at you!" He looked me up and down. His smile went weird when he looked at my hair.

I proudly introduced him to Ahjani and Audra. Audra told Royal that his house was very nice. He humbly thanked her, and then he asked me how college life was treating me. I told him that I was attending a junior college, working at Spunkmeyer's, and spending as much time as I could with Ahjani. Royal smiled, then he asked me why I went so far away just to go to a JC. I tried to keep the sadness out of my voice as I said I needed a change. He laughed and said I flew across the country to bring back someone from the Bay. Then he started asking me what my plan was and I didn't really have an answer. Ahjani said that hopefully we'd have a real plan once his future was determined. Ahjani had the plan; I didn't have anything but love for Ahjani.

After a while, Royal asked me why I was growing my hair out. He mimicked me rolling his neck and his eyes as he repeated to me what I said when he asked me why I cut all of my hair off. I told him I couldn't find work until I started growing my hair out. He told me I needed to come back out here if being out there meant I had to compromise so much. I told him it wasn't a big deal. Then he smiled and asked what was with the pink. Royal tried to get me to go outside of my color world of monotones and I fought him. I told him that the color looked good on me so I wear it. Royal looked at Ahjani, "and I guess you're behind the perfume too?"

"Royal, it was a gift." I said defensively.

"Un huh, just remember that you don't have to put up with anything. I have three extra bedrooms. You can have one whenever you need it. Call me whenever."

"Thank you Royal."

He frowned at Ahjani, "matter of fact I would like to hear how you're getting along weekly but I'll settle for biweekly."

"Royal?" I didn't understand what was going on.

"I can see you compromising a whole lot to be with this young man. I just hope he's worth it."

"Royal, Ahjani's a good guy. He loves me, he tells me, and he shows me. He shares everything he has with me and we're always together. He's good to me."

"Un huh, everything good to you isn't good for you."

"I understand sir, I'm happy she has someone in her corner. I love your daughter very much. I hope there would never be a time when she'd need to get away from me." Ahjani swallowed as he looked at me. "I have no intentions of hurting her."

Royal calmed down, then he told me that he's happy for me, but scared. He said young love can be volatile.

That night Ahjani started kissing my neck. I told him there was no way we were doing it in his mom's house. Ahjani looked shocked as he bucked his big eyes at me and asked me how we were supposed to last a week in each other's presence without him going in. I told him I didn't know but his mom was sleep probably lightly in the next room to make sure we wouldn't disrespect her. He said he'd be quiet, I told him he knew I couldn't say the same. He said he'd gag me. He laughed I didn't, I held on to my conviction. Then his hands went everywhere perfectly as he kissed me in all the right places. He put a towel on the bed and then we had our very first session of controlled sex. The faces Ahjani made as he tried to be quiet were hilarious. He put his hand over my mouth as he said, "purr for daddy!" I wonder if that's the magical words he uses to make my body explode.

In the morning I faked sleep cause even if they didn't hear us. They probably heard the bed. I couldn't look his mom in the face. When it got quiet in the house I got up. Ahjani and Ahjanae were sitting at the table drinking coffee and talking while Erin ate cereal in her high chair. Ahjanae said she really likes me. I smiled as I listened. Ahjani told his big sister that he loves me so much that lately he's become paranoid about me leaving him. Ahjanae told him I was a good egg and he had nothing to worry about. Then he told her about Spencer and Courtney. She left him and moved on to the next guy. Ahjanae asked questions about Courtney and then she said I wasn't anything like Courtney. Then he asked if I was like Nellie, and she said I wasn't stuck on myself. He defended her and said that wasn't how she really was. I'm guessing Nellie is the ex-girlfriend he mentioned the other night in his sleep right before he started calling out my name. I smiled as Ahjanae went down a list of reasons why I was better than the other girl. I guess they've been talking about me for some time. Ahjani agreed that I was ten times better. Then he said he wants to get a place for us. He said my best friend is scandalous and he doesn't want to be the reason we stop being friends. I guess this is why he hasn't been coming over and we've been getting so many hotel rooms. I tried not to deflate at the thought of him not telling me, or my only friend out there trying to push up on my man. I opened my bedroom door, closed it and then I went to the bathroom. I cried a little bit, threw some water on my face then I joined them in the kitchen. I was pouring my cup of coffee when Ahjanae cleared her throat. "If I would've known all I had to do was go away to college then it'd be ok to have sex in this house I would've done that."

I wanted to die and Ahjani choked on his coffee. "Yea mister nasty!" Audra said coming in the kitchen.

"You will never touch me again!" I screamed as I buried my head in his shoulder.

"I tried to be quiet," Ahjani's voice cracked. "You think

momma heard?"

I screamed and tried to bury my face further. "I'm gonna stay at my mom's! I can't look you guys in the face."

"I doubt she heard you. She was calling hogs. I barely heard the bed, but Ahjani's muffled moan was the giveaway. Gross!"

I screamed again, while Ahjani rubbed my back and laughed. "I'm a slave to catnip, what can I say?"

****

"You must be Ahjani, I'm Ms. Roth. It's nice to finally meet you." My mom said in a business tone.

"Yes I am, nice to meet you Ms. Roth." He smiled, "my family is all inside we were just waiting on you and this little man. How you doing?" He said to my little brother.

My little brother looked up to Ahjani with big eyes. "How did you get to be so tall?"

"I ate all my vegetables and I do what my momma tells me to."

"Wow!"

My mom and I hugged for the first time since before I left. "You're letting your hair grow out! You look good, Ahjani you got my baby in pink."

Ahjani looked at me, "did you hate pink or something?"

"It was never my favorite color."

"She hated it! Now look at you! It's a beautiful color on

you too."

Ahjani gave me a funny look then he opened the door to the restaurant. My mom tried to shake Aquilla's hand, but Aquilla bypassed her hand and hugged her anyways. Then Ahjani's Aunt Kharee did the same thing. My mom didn't get her handshake until she was introduced to Ahjani's uncle Jason. There was an extra chair and I asked Ahjani who it was for. He said for whenever his brother showed. As the waiter came around his brother walked in. I sunk in my seat! Shoot! Darn! Crap! NO WAY! His brother had his eyes locked on me as he walked. I could see my mom sizing him up and assigning him DBS status. Not that she was wrong, cause last I knew he was, this was not going to go over well with her. He nodded at Ahjani and then he nodded at me. His way of nonverbally asking who I was. Ahjani proudly introduced me to Aunrey. I said a guilty, "I know him."

"You didn't have to say nothing. I wasn't going to." Aunrey said looking at his menu.

"How you know my brother?" Ahjani didn't ask loudly. Since I was sitting next to my mom everything seemed amplified.

"He knows a guy I used to date."

Ahjani was satisfied with my answer and he dropped it. My mom on the other hand looked horrified. I could see her trying to keep the dragon lady away, but I knew she was going to go off as soon as she could.

****

"GET YOUR NARROW TAIL IN HERE NOW!" My mom yelled at me as soon as I got out the car.

I took a deep breath, I was happy Ahjani didn't come with me for this. I told him I needed to talk to my mom alone. He didn't

47

ask me any questions; he handed over the key to the rental car. "Where's my brother?" I closed the door behind me.

"With his father. Who's the guy?" She looked like she wanted to pounce on me.

"Mom, it's in the past. Please let it go."

She walked up in my face and started choking me. "You wanna live like ghetto people! I'll show you ghetto!" Normally she yells for a while before she lets the dragon lady out, I guess she held back as long as she could already.

I hit her with my hand, she let me go. I stumbled backwards. "Mom! Please!"

"We might as well have lived in Oakland for this element in our lives. All my hard work to raise you above the ghetto element and you run to it. You run around with thugs and Drive-By-Shooters. And don't get me started on your little boyfriend. All those ghetto cuckabugs all over the place. His Aunt is married to a DBS and his Aunt and all her girls got those big ole ghetto blaster booties! Teenage mother for a sister, and they all got different daddies. Who can even pronounce their names? Weaves and extensions all around the table! I had to take four showers to wash the ghetto off of me last night!"

"Ahjani comes from a good family."

She started swinging on me, hitting me in my head and back. "That ghetto hot mess is not a good family. You don't know nothing about a good family apparently. I've shown you good families." I moved out of her range of hitting on me. "Why are you hitting me? Because I'm not doing what you want me to do? You act like we live in Beverly Hills, this is Castro Valley. People are on welfare and live in low income housing here too. With all the bed hopping you do miss four divorces!" Since she was going to be mad at me anyways, I went there. "Last I checked, my brother and I do not have the same father. And my father had to have a DNA test to prove I was his after he took a look at one of your ex's. You have no right to judge people!" The dragon lady completely came over her and I ran! I ran out the door to the rental car. The car took me to Royal's house. I tried to pretend like I was ok, but one look at my eyes and Royal wanted to know what was wrong. When he hugged me I realized my back was tender. Royal asked me where Ahjani lived, and I told him I came from my mom's house. Royal put my brother and I in the car and he stood on the gas as he drove to my mom's house. I didn't want to go in, but he gently pulled me out the car. My mom stood in the doorway and told Royal to leave my brother, and to take me away. She said if he came near her house she was calling the police. Royal marched up to the door. My mom slammed the front door and you heard her lock it. Royal kicked the door in! My mom called 911! Royal cursed my mom out so badly I covered my little brother's ears. My mom's neighbor Mr. Lowe came over and he asked me if I was ok. He said he knew something was going to happen when he heard my mom screaming at me when I came originally. The police came fast and my mom said she wanted Royal arrested for trespassing. Royal told the officers that she beat on his nineteen-year-old daughter and he wanted her arrested. The female officer looked at me, then she said she didn't see evidence of abuse. Royal told me to take my jacket off. When I only moved my jacket a little the female officer saw a bruise on my back. My little brother started crying, and my mom said she didn't do it. She said I was lying on her. Mr. Lowe told Royal that he heard the argument but I left before he called the police. Ms. Roth just about lost it and she told Royal she would drop the trespassing charge and she wouldn't hold him accountable for the door. Royal told her to sign over custody of his son. She agreed as she begged him not to have her sent away.

Ahjani

Jason put the drape over me then he took out his comb. He kept looking at my eyes like he was waiting for me to come clean. "School's going very well."

"Good." He looked a little relieved. "The girl?"

"I love her, she's not pregnant." I knew that would take the stress lines off his face and it did. "The thing is that we need our own place." Jason looked at me as he combed my hair. "I know you feel I'm young and this might be too much for me to handle, but we dang near live together now. I figure with all the money I spend on hotels for us just to be alone it would be cheaper to rent a place."

"Ok," Jason said turning on his clippers.

"Ok? That's it?"

"Yep."

"Jason I had this whole speech prepared. I even thought about making charts to support my claims."

"We met her, she's a nice young lady. Your grades haven't slipped. You're still commanding on the court. We'll go over your new budget and how much of an apartment you can afford. I don't think you're going to completely mess this up."

"Completely?"

"You have that girl bending over backwards to make you happy."

"I bend for her too."

"Oh yea, how?"

I bounced my leg, "I'm faithful to her."

Jason chuckled, "you're faithful?" He spoke to his reflection in the mirror in front of us, "he's faithful he says." Then he chuckled again. "You're supposed to be faithful moron! Doing what you're supposed to do isn't an accomplishment. You haven't really been tempted yet. Mark my words; it's going to take losing her for you to understand what you had. For your sake, I hope she's a forgiving person."

"Jason, your niece is on line one." Tiffany called out from the receptionist desk.

Jason picked up the phone, "this is Jason... ok..." his eyes darted to me. " Hold on..." He brought the phone to me, "it's for you."

"Hello?"

"Thanks Ahjanae. Ahjani, I had Ahjanae call you on three-way." Olivia was trying to sound too calm. "My mom and I got into a fight, and Royal feels I'm too upset to drive by myself. He's insisting on driving me to your house. Do you think it would be too much trouble to ride with him back to pick up the car?" Her voice shook a little, "I'm so sorry for the inconvenience."

"It's not a problem. Since I'm at the barbershop do you think Royal would mind waiting until I get there?"

Olivia asked Royal and then he got on the phone. "Hey Ahjani, no problem at all. Olivia says you're in Oakland somewhere. We could drop off the key to you on the way to your place if it would be easier for you to get to the car from there. I'm thinking it's a shorter distance. You could catch Bart out here, it's a little walk, but the car is right outside my house."

"That's fine, is she ok?"

"She's going to be ok. Which barbershop are you at?"

"I'm at Drew's off of East 14th."

"Oh you mean International Blvd, they changed the name some years ago."

"Oh, I didn't even notice."

"Right, a street by any other name…. We'll swing by with the key in a minute. Then I'll take her to your house so she can rest."

"Sounds like a plan, thank you Royal." I gave the phone back to Jason.

Jason waited for me to say something, so I told him what they told me. Jason nodded his head, and then he said Royal wants to know where to find me when he comes looking for me. My house, where I get my haircut, a look at my family. He said he did the same thing to Omar. Little miss Olive tried to put on a smile as she sat in the car, but she was upset. It must've been a really bad argument. I kissed her and I told her I would be home in a little bit.

When Jason finished my hair cut he gave me a ride to Royal's place. He got out the car and walked boldly into his backyard. He walked around the house surveying everything. Then he opened the mailbox, he wrote down Royal's name and address. I asked Jason what was up, and he said it was standard practice to check out the father of the woman I loved. Then he followed me back to Richmond. When we got off the freeway he went to his home and I went to mine. Royal's truck was still parked out front. Royal was talking to my momma, and Audra and Olive's little brother were at the table eating cookies and milk. That little boy was looking at Audra with stars in his eyes, she didn't notice it.

"Hey son," my momma said as I kissed her cheek.

"I was telling your momma that Olivia and Judith had a pretty bad fight today. I didn't feel comfortable with her driving like that. I appreciate you being flexible."

"Why weren't you at the dinner last night?"

"I can't stand Judith, and she can't believe I don't cave in to her. She tries to keep me out of the loop as much as possible when it comes to my little girl."

"That and the fact that you aren't her biological father." I chimed in.

My momma seemed so touched; "my late husband took Ahjani and Ahjanae, my other daughter, under his wing just like that. You never would've known he wasn't their biological father by the way he was with them verses Audra. It takes a special kind of man to love children like that. I commend you." My momma said.

"Olivia's laying down?" I said walking towards my room.

"Yes, let me say goodbye so I can get going. Little man and I tried to convince Olivia to eat something with us, but she's too upset."

I opened my door and Royal went in. He rubbed Olivia's hair and kissed her forehead. He told her he would check on her tomorrow after he got off work. Then he left. I laid on the bed behind Olivia and when I scooted in to hold her from behind, she moaned a little in pain. Realizing she flinched, she jumped up and turned on the light in the room. I asked her what happened. Olivia thought about playing it cool for a minute then she turned her back to me and took off her sweater. Bruises were all over her back. Fire turned in my stomach, "what happened?"

Olivia talked above her tears as she said her momma got mad because her ex-boyfriend was a "thug." She tried to standup for herself then she ran away on autopilot to Royal's house. She said Royal's taking her little brother to stay with him. She explained that her momma thinks because she's got a little money and always has men in her life who have money that she's above anything ghetto, when in actuality everything about her life was ghetto. Her mother had a rotating door of men, do as I say not as I do. Even though her parents were barely married her father needed proof that she was his kid. Her momma cheated on Royal, which is why he can't stand her. I held on to Olive and I told her I was sorry I wasn't there to protect her.

Chapter 5

Olivia

It felt good to be able to tell Ahjani about the dragon lady. I told him everything. Purging like that, although difficult made me feel lighter, but terrible at the same time. I felt like I was betraying my mom. Ahjani and I spent that night purging. He talked about his father, something he never does. Our fathers were pretty similar, they barely existed. He told me about his stepfather, and how he was a lot like Royal. He said in honor of his stepfather, he spoils Audra rotten; she's his last link to a man who showed him what love should look like. He said his step father was good to his mom, and he knew she misses him.

That night was the first night we talked about our future together. Ahjani told me again how much he loves me and needs me in his life. I told him he was really stuck with me now. I told him that was scary for me to love anyone as much as I loved him. That night our bond became stronger.

On the plane Ahjani held my hand and stroked it while looking out the window at the clouds. "Don't you wish you could live up here? I bet life up in the clouds is pretty peaceful."

"I never wondered what life up here would be like."

"Let's imagine it for a minute." He rested his head on his headrest. "Ok, close your eyes what do you see?"

I closed my eyes and saw fluffy white clouds and a little ways away dark and ugly storm clouds. "I see birds soaring, without a care in the world."

"Yeah, this is their space right. They are the master of these skies, we all visit."

"Yes, but we're not invited guest, so I can imagine that birds get angry when we pass through."

He chuckled, "we make birds angry?"

"I think so, ever since man took to the skies we've interrupted the one place they could go to escape us. No peace on the ground and now no peace in the skies."

"So when we think they're soaring having a nice flight, they're trying to attack us?"

"Yes! I like that. All the planes that have crashed for no reason have been because of the bird's secret attack on the planes. The monsters of the skies."

Ahjani started laughing, "I love how you changed my place of peace and tranquility to a war zone." He rubbed my hand, "it's ok."

"Sorry, I did do that didn't I?"

"It's ok, I understand why." He laughed a little. "I wanna ask you something, and please remember you always have the right to tell me no." I looked at him, he looked a little nervous. "As the first step towards the rest of our lives will you move in with me?"

I smiled, "you want to live with me?"

"More than I want to play basketball." He watched my eyes for an answer.

"I would love to!" Then I kissed him.

Ahjani smiled with relief, "let's keep this between us until we actually move in."

"Why? I'll need to give Julia a heads up that I'll be leaving so we can settle the bills."

"I understand that, but I know she isn't going to be happy for you. I was hoping we could avoid the drama for a minute."

"How do you know that?" I wanted to know what was going on.

He took a deep breath. "My ex was the first female to like me without all the hype. I was just Ahjani, the skinny, big eyed kid with the name people always messed up. Once they noticed me on the court I became **Ahjani Lubbock** the star!" He laughed, "girls come from all over to see if the rumors are true. Most of them didn't even bother to give me their name. All of them have that hungry for me look in their eyes. It's never love. All the Courtney's of the world. Julia is always looking at me with that same look. That's why I don't go to your place unless I'm with you, and I avoid her as much as I can."

"A look doesn't mean she won't be happy for me."

"She tries to find excuses to touch me or be around, but you're probably right. Maybe I don't know what I'm saying."

"Is there anyone else you were thinking of sparing their feelings? Like Fiona?"

He blew air, "no! She's doing her own thing. I don't cheat on you."

****

"This is amazing!" I said taking in our small apartment building.

Ahjani put his arms around me, "it's good to see you smile again." He kissed my cheek.

Ahjani called me this morning to tell me our application was approved. We just signed our lease. Our move in date was in one week. "What are we going to do about summer?"

"We'll put our furniture in storage, go home, then we'll come back and do it again. Let's have a celebratory dinner. Where you wanna go?"

"The mall, I want to get an idea for what we'll need."

"I don't think we should get anything too nice. It's going to be in and out of storage over the next three years. Let's keep it simple."

"Simple?"

"Yea, like IKEA simple."

"IKEA has nice stuff."

"Ok, but you understand what I mean."

"Yea," I tried not to sound disappointed.

He smiled, "we will need a good bed though."

"Let's go!" I drug him to the mall.

Ok so the first bed I liked was really girly. Ahjani protested more than I thought he would. We found a suitable compromise. Ahjani paid for it and we scheduled the delivery for the day after we got our keys. We bought a lot of bedding cause Ahjani said we'd definitely need it.

When Ahjani and I walked in the door with all of our bags, I immediately felt bad when I saw Julia and her man sitting on the couch. "Shopping spree?"

I smiled and hoped she'd be happy for me. "Guess what! Ahjani asked me to move in with him!" I covered my mouth as I smiled.

Julia stared at me for a minute without saying anything. "You barely work, how can you afford to do that?"

"We're going to make it work."

"I don't think it's a good idea to rely on him to support you. What if he changes his mind?"

"You're going to stop being my friend when I move out?"

"I'm not going to give you money. I pay most of the bills here. I think you're setting yourself up."

"Good thing this is our choice." Ahjani said, "I'll take these bags with me." He kissed me, "see you tomorrow."

My feelings were hurt so I got in the bed. I told myself to find a better job in the morning.

****

"You look familiar," the lady blurted out in the middle of my interview. She started clicking on her computer. "YEP, it's you." She turned her monitor so I could see it. One of the pictures I took with Ahjani during Julia's practice shoot was on her screen.

"Oh yes, my friend Julia Blake is a very talented photographer. I've assisted her on a lot of her shoots. She's on my resume. Her models for that shoot backed out at almost the last minute so my boyfriend and I filled in."

"I like you Olivia. My only drawback is figuring out the summer. Summer and Spring are typically busy times for me." She put her fingers to her mouth. "Still, you are my first likeable candidate. What to do? What to do?" She picked up her camera and snapped a few shots. "I have a couple of other interviews today. I'll call by the end of the week."

"Even if you don't choose me it was nice meeting you Paula." I said as I stood.

When I got home Ahjani was studying. I kissed his forehead, then I went to the closet in our bedroom. I pulled out my camcorder, then I told Ahjani I'd be back. I wandered around the park filming squirrels, birds, and trees. "Olivia?"

It was Spencer, "hey! How you feeling?" I gave him a hug.

He looked depressed and sad. "Just came from physical therapy. I'm healing pretty well. What are you doing?"

"Playing a game. I'm trying to capture a mood. I'll put music to it."

"And then?"

I shrugged, "I don't know. My best friend and I used to play this game all the time."

"Will you walk with me? I gotta do two more laps around this park."

"Sure." I said

I captured more footage as we walked around the park. Spencer offered to drive me home, but I declined cause we lived nearby. Ahjani was cooking when I came home. I told him I ran into Spencer at the park. Ahjani listened then he said he felt bad for him.

Ahjani

I cursed when the phone rang. My early morning dose of catnip had me knocked out like I didn't just sleep eight hours. "Hello?"

"Hello, yes this is Paula Giovinale. May I speak to Olivia."

"One moment," I held the phone up as I kissed Olive's neck. "Baby Paula's on the phone."

Olive sat up and took the phone. "Hello?....... Yes........ Yes........ I understand....... Ok......, thank you!" She reached over me to put the phone back in the cradle. Since she put it in my face I sucked her nipple in. "Don't start!" She warned. "I got the job!" She screamed excitedly.

I rubbed her stomach, "we've got to celebrate!"

"There's only one problem. She looked at me, I gotta be out here most of the summer."

I sucked my teeth, "what?"

"I guess we could downsize for the summer still. I could rent a room or studio somewhere until you come back." I let the disappointment show on my face. "Please be ok with this Ahjani. This job is going to do wonders for my resume."

"A whole summer without catnip? You must want me to go blind!"

"Think of it as an away game. We can do this."

I backed away from her, "give me some time to be selfish. I'll come around."

She got on top of me, "she's going to have gigs in LA maybe you could drive out." She kissed my neck.

I surprised myself as I responded to her kiss. She looked at me in disbelief. "I'm just as surprised as you are."
****

FRUSTRATED! I met with my academic advisor and it appears that I've wasted time in a few of the wrong classes. With a heavy class load I could make up the time in six months instead of a year if I buckle down. I was so upset when I came home. Little miss Olive Oil assured me that it would be ok and we could manage to make this happen. If I decided to go Pro, this derailment would still cost me a year regardless.

****

I just finished my run, school was almost over and instead of enjoying my time with little miss Olive Oil like my momma told me to. I've been panicking and overdosing so much on catnip that the kitty is now out of commission for seven of the longest days of my life. I don't want to leave without her. Ahjanae says I have a ridiculous case of separation anxiety. I've gone so far as to tag along with her to work. Olive is an assistant to Paula Giovinale, a pretty major photographer. Julia was blatantly jealous when Olive tried to mention it in passing. Paula is very laid back and reasonable. She smiles at us and says she remembers young love. Paula is single and she lives in a big and beautiful house. She's offered my Olive a place to stay during the summer. Olive was going to say no, but I convinced her to take Paula up on her offer. She'd be a fool to think she could go back to Julia's, and I wouldn't worry about her being alone.

I took a long chug on my water. "Lubbock, what's up?"

It was Spencer, just like Olive says he doesn't look happy anymore. "What's up man? You doing pretty good. You out here running?"

"Yea, I'm at about seventy-five to eighty percent back. It's going to take some time if I ever get back to one hundred percent." He shook his head as he looked around. "My moms tried to warn me, but I didn't listen. I got caught up in all the hype. Now...." He shook his head.

"I'm sorry man, I know it has to be hard."

"The poor man's dentist HUH?"

"Yes sir, especially after watching your life unfold I'm leaning more that way."

"Olivia doesn't try to convince you to stick to the game? She doesn't want to be a basketball wife?"

"Nope, we've been planning for dental schools after graduation. I'm going to do that in California."

"Congratulations, you've got a good woman." He looked hurt.

"What you doing tonight?"

"Nothing."

"Olivia's friend is coming over for dinner. I would appreciate having someone to talk to while they talk about pictures and videos."

"I can supply the alcohol."

"That's cool, come early; five-thirty."

Olive said we'd have enough food to accommodate everyone. I stood there looking at her, Olive said we had one more day. Then she served me up nicely. Head is cool to take the edge off, but nothing beats catnip.

Spencer dang near bought out the liquor store. He brought a box full of liquor. He mixed drinks for us, by the time Julia got there she had three drinks waiting for her just to get on our level. Olive had her pictures and video setup and ready. Julia gulped her first two drinks, then she sipped her third as she setup. Julia told Spencer he was automatically on her side cause I couldn't be trusted to be impartial. Spencer was open to her flirting with him, but he wasn't falling all over himself either. We voted on the pictures that captured the visual of the songs they chose. Olive was a lot better at this than she gave herself credit for. I didn't know she took a picture of me when I was sitting in the couch going through catnip withdrawals. I was leaning forward, hands clasped, with my head drooping forward. It was black and white and I looked stressed. She wrote anxiety on the back and the music made it seem like I was disquieted within my thoughts. Julia looked at the picture and asked Olive if she was pregnant. I spit my drink while Olivia held up her drink and told her to get real. Olive told her she wasn't having any babies until she was married, I smiled again. We had a nice evening listening to the girls speak to their work. I couldn't understand most of it cause I was extremely tipsy. It got late and Spencer was too twisted to drive and Julia wasn't going to leave, it was too late. Olive and I were cuddling when there was a gentle knock on the door. I cracked the door and Spencer asked me for a condom. I gave it to him then I got back in the bed. Olive laughed and said as soon as the liquor started pouring she knew that was going to happen. I asked Olive when Julia and her man broke up. Olive exhaled and then she said as far as she knew they were still together. She said Julia doesn't really like him, and that she was only with him until the summer. Next year it would be the next guy. I asked why she didn't wait until she found someone she really liked or possibly even loved. Olive said they had that argument all the time. She said Julia gets impatient, and she didn't want to be single waiting for something to happen that may never. I asked her how she dealt with that while she was single. Olive said she liked me from the moment she met me. Then she shrugged and said it was fine as long as she could admire me from a far. I thought about when I met her. She had NO HAIR! The thought didn't even cross my mind that I could've even been interested in her.

****

We moved all of our major items to storage. Then we drove to Paula's place. I was spending my last two nights here and then Olive was keeping my car while I was out in California.

Paula made a big fuss over me being here and welcoming Olive. She had a special dinner prepared by a personal chef for the three of us. Then she had a private service come and give Olive and I full body table massages side by side on her deck overlooking her property. Then she put a bottle of champagne in Olive's room to cap the night off. I couldn't even pronounce the name, the bottle was so fancy. Olive's room was bigger than our apartment. I told her she was going to end up not ever wanting to come home after living it up with Paula. Olive assured me that wasn't possible because she would always want to be wherever I am. Olive and I properly broke that room in and we stayed captive in there for most of the next day. We only came out for food, and Paula had our meals waiting for us. I had a cab come take me to the airport cause I didn't want to have to walk away from Olive at the airport. When the plane started pulling away from the airport I put my headphones on and sucked it up. I was going to meet Olive in LA in two weeks. I took a deep breath I can do this.

Chapter 6

Olivia

Julia smiled at me as she thought about it. She said she liked Spencer and he was better in bed than her ex-boyfriend, but they were not in a committed relationship. He was free to do as he liked. "So what kind of mischief are you getting into this summer without your constant shadow?"

"Ahjani is not my shadow. I don't want mischief around me."

"Goodness! He's only been gone one day, you can't be backed up already."

Thank goodness the phone rang. "You've reached Paula Giovinale's assistant how may I help you?"

"I NEED YOU!" Ahjani yelled into the phone.
I smiled, "I have Paula's schedule in front of me. She has business to conduct in Hollywood. Can I put you on the agenda at that time?"

"My plane arrives ten minutes before yours. This will be the longest two weeks ever!"

Julia walked out the room shutting the door behind her. I exhaled, "I miss you so much!" I touched my hair. "Oh I need to warn you that my hair will be braided by the time I see you."

He sucked his teeth. "Why?"

"It's too hot and humid out here. I don't have time to deal with it. You're not here to play with it so I'm putting it up."

"You always got excuses. You should wear your hair with honor. Everyone can't grow their hair like you can and you want to throw it away."

"Jani baby, I don't want to spend our time arguing about stupid hair. It's an accessory." I know he hates when I say that but it's true. Some people assign too much value to hair.

"Fine! Can you at least send me a picture before you bind it all up?"

"Whatever," sometimes I wonder if my hair would be grounds for breaking up with me. "Julia said Spencer wants me to go out with him tonight. Is that ok with you?"

"I'm clearly not your daddy!"

I smiled, "you're not ?"

He laughed, "well I am but I'm not. You know what I mean. Just make sure he doesn't switch focus."

"Please he has Julia. She's not as bad as Courtney but I can see them going further."

Paula and I went over her agenda for the next couple of days. I looked at the clock, I told her I was going out with Spencer and Julia tonight, I asked her if she wanted to go. She reluctantly said no, and I convinced her to come. She excitedly said ok, then she said we could take her Mercedes. I called Julia and I told her we'd pick her up. I got so excited when Paula passed me the keys. This car was ridiculous! I melted into the leather, then I took a minute to adjust the mirrors to suit my needs. Paula laughed then she said I could drive any of her cars whenever I liked since I was so cautious. "How long have you and Julia been friends?"

"Since we were kids."

"I know you have to decide for yourself, but be careful with her. She's out for herself."

I wanted to ask her how she knew that but I didn't. I used the car phone to tell her to come down. Spencer smiled and Julia screamed when I rolled my window down and asked them if they wanted a ride. Paula gave Spencer a seductive smile when I introduced them. Julia tried to pretend like she didn't care, but I could tell it bothered her.

When we got to the club we got in line, and Paula told us to follow her. The guy at the door let us float in, he didn't even card us. Julia and I were nervous about the whole ID issue. We found a table and then Spencer took our drink orders then he went to the bar.

Paula asked Julia what her status was with Spencer. Julia tried to be normal when she said he was free to do what he wants. Paula asked Julia if she minds if she took him home tonight. I knew it was a test, Julia looked away and said she didn't care. I was speechless! Even Julia tries to say she's not into Spencer like that, I know better. I think Paula intimidates her, I don't know why else she would back down like this.

A guy asked Julia to dance and then Spencer came back with our drinks. He spotted Julia on the dance floor then he sat down. Paula started flirting with Spencer immediately. A guy came out and greeted Paula, he thanked her for coming. Then he moved us to his booth in the VIP section. Paula kept telling everyone who

Spencer is and highlighting who he was. They'd say tough break then they'd ask him if he was going to continue playing. He said he wasn't sure. At Paula's subtle encouragement everyone was pumping Spencer's head up. As he sat there feeling good about himself Paula pulled him in for a kiss. A guy invited me to dance, as I walked on the dance floor Julia helplessly watched them kiss at the table. I apologized cause I felt guilty. Julia turned her back and said she didn't care as she danced harder with her partner. I had a good time dancing, as the night wore on and people got more drunk one guy got too happy with his hands. When I attempted to walk away he grabbed my hand like he wasn't going to let me walk away. Spencer came out of nowhere and he asked me if I was ok. The guy let me go, then Spencer asked me to dance with him. His eyes were droopy from all the drinks. "Julia left with some guy."

"You ok?"

"I'm fine, are you ok?"

"Yes of course. I wish Ahjani was here."

"He'll be back soon enough." Then the song went off.

Paula asked Spencer if he was coming back to the house with us for a nightcap. He told her he needed to get his car from Julia's then he'd follow us. When we got in Paula's car they got in the back. I felt like the driver in an episode of taxicab confessions or something. They were making out all over the backseat of her car. Spencer groaned and said he'd get his car tomorrow, Paula tapped my chair and told me to take us home. I knew my face was red behind listening to them. Paula told me to keep the keys as I got out of her car. I ran to my room and shut my door. I called Ahjani and we laughed together as I gave him a play by play of my night.

In the morning, I was up showered and dressed in the kitchen with the housekeeper Lily as she made breakfast and told me about her crazy son. Spencer walked in the kitchen shirtless with passion marks all over his neck and chest. I introduced Spencer to Lily, who looked at Spencer with big eyes. I guess Paula won't mind him walking around half naked, her way of showing of her conquest I guess. I turned my eyes, all I could think about was the fun they had. Paula came out in her robe and she looked happily hung over. Paula asked what her agenda looked like for next weekend. When I told her she told me to clear her

Friday afternoon through Monday night. Then she picked up Spencer's hand and kissed it. She told me to book a trip for her and Spencer to Miami. Then she told him she'd see him later and that I had her keys to take him to his car after he ate. When Paula went back to her room Lily and I smiled at Spencer. He blushed and told us to leave him alone. I didn't say anything I enjoyed my expensive coffee.

"You think Julia's mad?"

I kept my eyes on the road. "I don't know."

"Would you be mad?"

"If you were Ahjani none of that would've happened. Are you two together?"

"No, not exactly. Courtney didn't care about stuff like this. She even invited a couple girls to join us before." I exhaled hard, "did that feel like love to you?"

Spencer laughed, "at the time it did. I felt like she loved me enough not to sweat the small stuff."

"I wouldn't tell Julia anything outside of the obvious about Ahjani. I don't want anyone looking at him like I see him. When it's love you won't want to share."

"I guess my girl before Courtney was my last shot at love. She was heartbroken when we broke up. I couldn't see it then. It's too late to apologize."

"Spencer it's never too late to apologize. Hopefully she's moved on with her life and she's happy. However, hearing a person you loved at one point in your life apologize is worth gold."

Spencer stared at me for a minute. "Who was he?"

"Stupid ex, he constantly cheated, even had babies on me!" It still hurt like it was seconds ago.

Spencer whispered, "he went bare back too. That's too bad."

I parked, "I'm going to go up and check on her. Make sure she's ok."

"Me too."

Julia opened the door in her robe and she had been crying. She said the guy she left with tried to rape her in an alley. She managed to get out of the car, but he had her purse so she couldn't call anyone for help. She walked to a cafe where she called the police and the officer gave her a ride home. She said the officer was nice and stayed with her while she waited for her apartment manager who changed her locks. I hugged her and cried with her. Spencer went in her kitchen he said he'd make her something to eat. He told her she had no food, I had to get back to Paula, Spencer said he'd stay with her.

When I told Paula what happened to Julia, she felt bad for her. She told me to invite Julia on the shoot the Tuesday after she came back from her trip with Spencer.

****

"The waiter came while you were in the bathroom, so I ordered for you." Spencer said nonchalantly.

"How do you know what I like?"

"Whenever we come here you order the same thing, eggs Benedict, fruit cup instead of potatoes and a large glass of freshly squeezed orange juice. Am I wrong?" He asked Paula.

"Olivia you are somewhat a creature of habit on something's. That's also what makes you dependable." She said as she looked over her contract. "How's Julia?" She didn't look up.

"Same as before." Spencer replied.

"Olivia sweetie where is her family? Why aren't they reaching out to her?"

"Her mother's in California, and she and her dad aren't close. I doubt he even knows where she lives. She has other family but she isn't close to any of them."

"So that just leaves you two to help her." Then she put her contract down. "That was a pretty cool little game you two played the other day. You say you've done that since you were children?"

"Yes, it was how we kept the phone bill down."

"Your work is amazing." She locked her eyes on mine.

"Naw, this has always been Julia's game."

"You may have let her facilitate the game, but that was your game. You are good! What do you want to do with your talent?"

"Whatever will pay the bills really."

"Here's what you're going to do. You're going to transfer over to the university and I'll show you what classes you need to take. Meanwhile, knowing that you possess such talents, I cannot in good conscience let you continue on as a mere assistant. I want to offer your job to Julia. I've decided that you will be my associate. You're going to be my instead of. When I can't be somewhere that I'm needed you will go instead. You have a good eye, and this is your calling. Of course this means that I will have to pay you a lot more than you make now." Then she looked at Spencer, "we can discuss money later."

"Paula…" I was speechless!

"Don't go all girl on me and start crying or something like that. A simple thank you will do."

I got up and rushed her with a hug, and I kissed her cheek. "THANK YOU PAULA!"

"The rest of this summer I will coach you, and then when I feel you're ready you will go out and make me proud."

Ahjani

This summer was weird, it drug on and then it would speed up when I'd get to see Olive. I worked at the dental office that I worked in during high school. Everyone was so excited to see me and hear about college life. When Olive surprised me by showing up there all I heard after that was how pretty she was and how I picked a good one. Then the hygienist said she was definitely my type. I asked what she meant and she said Olive was like the other girlfriend I had. I asked Maritza if all black people look the same to her. Kind of rude I know but she put me in a bad mood. So I asked my sisters if they thought Olivia was like Nellie. They said there were some similarities but they're two totally different people. I spent that night thinking about Nellie, wondering what really happened to her. How could she let her parents keep her away from me? Did she even love me like she said she did? Or was she the original Thing 1 and my mind just couldn't see it? I thought about her so much and so hard that I kept dreaming about her. In my dreams she was full of apologies and explanations. **THEN** my original dose of the *catnip*…. With her I learned everything I know about sex today. She wasn't afraid to try anything, and the more adventurous I was the happier she was. Nellie, *Nealesha* was my first love, my first heartbreak, and the first _real_ thing in my life. Her home life was messed up, but whose isn't? She would put on like she didn't care what people thought of her or even that she liked being difficult, but I knew better. She couldn't pull that junk with me. If she thought I was upset with her, her whole world fell apart. I can still smell her perfume. I did buy it for Olive, but her body chemistry is different. I still love the smell on Olive, but it smells different, it's like it's not even the same fragrance. I've also gotten off Olive's case about wearing pink since I picked up on the fact that she doesn't really like the color. And the long hair, in my defense I like long hair on girl's period, it's not because of Nellie. She happened to have long hair that always smelled delicious. I spent the rest of my time in the Bay debating with myself. My brain had become suddenly infected with Nellie, I needed her gone. I was going home in a week to Little Miss Olive Oil. My Olive who is faithful and good to me.

****

My heart fluttered when I saw her. I don't know why I thought she was going to be wearing those God-awful braids when she picked me up. The first thing I did was put my hands in her hair and kiss her like I've missed her. She had a luggage cart for my bags. When she chirped a Mercedes in the parking garage I looked at her. She said it was Paula's and she let her drive her car all summer. She wanted to pick me up in style. She said my car was safe and sound in Paula's garage. Then she handed me the keys she said Paula told her it was ok to let me drive. We loaded up the trunk and backseat, when I sat in the driver's seat Olive smiled at me giving me a knowing smile. This car was nice and it glided, I tried not to enjoy the ride as much as I did. Along the way to Paula's, Olive told me that there were a few properties that Paula suggested that we look at and apply to if we liked them. She said Paula called the landlords personally to vouch for us. I asked her what that meant, and she said most likely they were really nice places. I reminded her that we didn't have a huge budget for a place, and she nodded and said she knew. Then she smiled, she said that Paula gave her a raise. When I asked what that meant, she said that we could still save like we planned and still live a little nicer than we were. I told her I didn't mind paying for everything, and she said she could never thank me enough. However, now she felt like a contributing member in our partnership. When we got to Paula's I noticed Spencer's car. Olive said Spencer spends his time between Julia and Paula these days. She said Julia's still kind of shaken up about the rape ordeal and even though she moved and everything she still gets pretty scared. Olive said she would go stay with her sometimes when she was really scared, or Paula would send Spencer.

When we walked in the door Spencer was on the couch shirt off entwined with Paula who had a glass of wine in her hand.

Apparently this was usual behavior in the house. "Ahjani! So good to see you! We were about to get in the hot tub, you two coming?"

Olive shook her legs, "um. Thank you Paula but we've got some other things to handle first."
Paula laughed, "young love! I remember it well. Try to come up for air at some point so we can share a meal together."

Olive started untucking her shirt and almost stripping before we were in the room good. We never made it to the bed, but we were all over that room like last time. I was gasping for air, "you've been working out I see."

"I had to do something I was going crazy!" She pushed her hair back. "This summer was long!"

"Too long, seeing you once a month was better than three months without you. But it was too long." I kissed her back. The camera on the tripod pointed at the bed caught my attention. "What were you doing?"

She smiled, "not what you're thinking. We were doing mock catalog shots. The lighting was better in here so I did some bedspread pictures. She got up and got the camera, then she showed me her pictures." Then she smiled. "I took some pictures for you on my camera, would you like to see them?"

"OF COURSE!" I sat up happy!

She got her camera then she sat in my lap. She leaned against me. Then she showed me each picture and she didn't change it until I asked her for the next one. At first it was just count down pictures until she saw me again. Then the pictures got more and more risky. I held her breast and massaged them as she showed me more. The more she showed me the more I touched her, then she asked me if I wanted to make a video. My eyes got big. I asked her if she was going to "leak it" to the public if I ended up being a NBA player. She shook her head no, she said that the video would only be for our eyes only. I asked her if she wanted to roll play or just get down to it. She said for this video was for us, if we did it again we could consider costumes and acting. She set up the camera and I washed up so did she. She broke her confident role to giggle a nervous laugh, then she said she was ready. She turned the camera on and the red light called action. As soon as she joined me on the bed I forgot about the camera. I made love to Olive, long hard, and passionately. In the morning we watched the play back, which only got us going again. Olive kept pointing out all the things she loved about my body, and how I wasn't afraid to be seen. I knew that was a comparison, but ask me if I care. I was winning so why would it matter?

****

Paula's name was golden, we got this extremely nice three bedroom townhouse for a little more than what we paid for our first one bedroom apartment. Even though Olive wanted to go crazy and furnish this place with nice things. I told her we still needed to live minimally cause we weren't staying in Georgia.

Ever since Julia's near pillaged experience, she doesn't look at me the same anymore. I wonder how it feels to share her man with a woman two times her age.

Chapter 7

Olivia

"Ahjani is going to meet us at the bowling alley. Let's go." Spencer said trying to hurry me out the door.

"When I talked to him this morning he said he was meeting me here at the studio. When did you talk to him?"

Spencer's eyes moved around the room. He's Paula's boy toy, and Julia's friend with benefits but he follows me around. Lately he says and does little things that make me feel a little uncomfortable. Ahjani has noticed it as well. He hasn't said anything to me about it, but there's underlying hostility between them now. I feel bad cause they used to be cool. They still get along, but its moments like this that make me want to ask him what is wrong with him. But I'm afraid of what his response could be. "Maybe I misunderstood."

"You don't have to wait with me, Ahjani will be here in a minute and then I'll ride over with him."

"I don't want to get there before you do. Paula's going to be in work mode, bossing me around. At least if you're there she'll leave the direction to you, and you have a nicer way of asking for what you want."

Julia walked into my office; she went down the list of things that have been confirmed for my shoot. I was happy she was in here when Ahjani got here, even though it didn't go unnoticed by Ahjani that Spencer looked real comfortable in his seat in front of my desk. I was editing pictures on my computer. "Hey baby!" I made sure I gave Ahjani a big kiss so it could never be confused that my loyalty has never wavered. Even though Ahjani played beautifully last night, I could tell that the loss was still messing with him. He was so upset he refused me, which was a first. He did seem a little distracted, but so did everyone else. Last night was not a good night for the whole team. Normally when they lose Ahjani is pretty positive about it. He's realistic enough to know he can't win every game, however last night for whatever reason it's messing with him. "You look good." I smiled.

"Thank you," then he stared at Spencer. "I need to talk to you, man to man." Julia looked at me and I started to walk out to give them space. "No, you two stay. I need to understand something. What happened this summer while I was away?"

"What do you mean?" Julia said crossing her arms and wrapping them around herself.

"When I leave, you two are hooked up, and Spencer you were my friend. Now, Julia's your side chick. You living like a kept man under Paula, when we all know you don't need her money or pampering. Then when my girl is at my game you constantly trying to stay in her ear. I may be on the court, but I got eyes. I've been waiting for someone to say something, but everyone's walking around here like they got blinders on."

Ahjani looked from person to person, and we all looked thoughtful. Ahjani looked like he was about to get irritated. "Baby I can't speak for what's happening with them. All I know is I'm in love with you, and only you. Anyone who tries to come between us is asking for an immediate rejection."

Ahjani looked at Spencer, "I'm only going to tell you this once. Don't cross me! I will come for you!"

Spencer stood up looked Ahjani up and down. "The thing is, I don't have to cross you. You're going to mess this up eventually. You're right, I could stand to ease up though."

I frowned, but I didn't want to ask him what he meant. Ahjani didn't ask him what he meant either, he told him to take his negativity somewhere else.

****

Julia ran to the bathroom barely making it to the toilet in time. Paula stopped talking and watched her door for Julia's return. When Julia returned I stood up, "Are you sick?" I said as I felt her forehead.

"I think I've got that bug that's been going around. I can hardly keep anything down." Julia said feeling her forehead.

"How long has this been going on?" Paula asked looking at Julia sternly.

"Just the other day. I could've picked this cold up anywhere. Probably at fashion week."

Paula gave Julia a tisking look, then she took her glasses off. She rubbed her eyes like she was tired, "are you pregnant?" Julia's mouth fell open like she didn't consider that as an option. "Look little girl, either you are or you aren't. I don't have all day to play these games with you."

Paula was direct and no nonsense about everything when it came to Julia. No sympathy or compassion for her or the fact that she took her man. Well kind of sort of her man. Julia sat down and looked down at her hands, "I don't know." She said it like she was in trouble with her mother.

"Is it...." She looked up at the ceiling, "what am I saying? Of course it's a possibility, you two still have sex. You need to take a test."

"Ok," Julia said looking around the room sadly.

Paula got impatient, "why aren't you going? Go to the store and get a test. Let's get this out of the way now, there's no sense in prolonging it."

Julia cleared her throat, I could tell she was trying to bite her tongue. "Thank you, but I'll wait to do all that tonight."

Paula looked at Julia, "you are such a little spoiled brat kid. What happened, mommy and daddy weren't getting along? They divorced and shattered your world? Instead of letting their messed up relationship be theirs, you've got a chip on your shoulder."

"Why don't you like me Paula? What did I ever do to you?"

Paula smiled at her, "I don't like you. I don't like the way that you are. I can still appreciate the fact that you have talent, and with proper grooming you could go somewhere. But you my dear think too much of yourself. I mean what did you think would happen? You leave the club with some guy you don't know, who you've just spent however much time freaking all night long. Was it the fact that he was trying to screw you in a car that freaked you out? Cause honestly I don't see how you thought the night was going any other way."

"You're just mad because Spencer still comes to me."

"Why would I care who that little boy screws? When you tell him you're pregnant, mark my words. He's going to tell you to get rid of it. If you're smart, you'll do as you're told. I don't know why you would even play with your body by allowing yourself to get pregnant. Rookie mistake little girl." Julia started crying, Paula put her hand up to her mouth. She bucked her eyes at Julia, "PLEASE DO NOT TELL ME YOU LOVE HIM!" Julia cried harder! "YOU IDIOT! THAT LITTLE BOY DON'T LOVE YOU!

Please tell me what has he done to make you love him? Sex is just sex!"

I felt bad for Julia, I handed the tissue box to her so she could wipe her nose. "Do you think you're pregnant?"

"Now that she said it, YES!" She cried so hard she couldn't talk for a minute. "I was changing birth control."

"Why would you have unprotected sex with someone who you're not in a committed relationship with?" Paula asked her in a condescending tone.

"I feel bad enough, you're only making me feel worse."

Paula looked at me like her patience was running thin. "I'M DONE! We're done for today! Olivia take my car, take her to the drug store to seal her fate. Take her home. You can keep my car overnight. I need to go smoke, this little tramp has thoroughly worked my nerves."

When we went to the drug store I bought two different kinds of test for her. She took them and they all said YES! Julia started freaking out asking me what she was going to do. I told her she needed to talk to Spencer. Julia said she knew she was in this by herself, she needed to decide what she was going to do. I told her to talk to him anyways.

All the way home my hands were sweating. I mean I'm on the pill, but Ahjani and I don't use condoms anymore. The thought of ending up pregnant before we were ready for it was a no go. Ahjani was sitting on the couch watching our video like he often does. He said he was never into porn, however he loves watching us. He says I'm beautiful to him when I cum, and he says we look good together. I told him when we watch that video all I do is look at him and remember how good he feels. Ahjani asked me why I was home so early. I told him I wanted to catch him in the act with his girlfriend on the screen. When he came in for a kiss he told me I was just in time. I barely kissed him back, then he asked me what was wrong. When I told him that Julia was pregnant, he turned off the movie and flopped down on the couch cause the mood was killed. I told him everything Paula said, and he said she could've said it nicer, but she didn't lie.

"What if we accidentally ended up pregnant?"

Ahjani slapped his forehead as if he had a brain freeze. "We would deal with it together."

"Would you want to get rid of it?"

"That's hard because we're not ready for babies yet. On the other hand, I don't know that I could ever ask you to go through with an abortion."

I relaxed a lot when he said that, "I think we should use condoms too. That way we're both doing our part to protect our futures."

Ahjani

She has to know it drives me insane when she does that! We're supposed to be studying and she keeps pushing hair to the other side of her head cause it's in her way. She pushes it to the left and then it gently falls, then she pushes it to the right and the same thing happens. I thought I loved her hair straight until one day she wore it curly. I can't keep my hands out of her hair. When she wears it curly she washes it frequently. So it always smells freshly washed and delicious. I can't even focus on schoolwork anymore. All I can think about is putting my hands in her hair and she has no idea. As the debate to continue studying has me stuck, her phone rang. On the phone she kept pushing all that hair some more. SHE'S TRYING TO KILL ME! DEAD AND BURIED! "HUH?" Did she just invite someone over? Did she not pick up on the "DO-ME" vibe I was kicking to her? "Julia is going to come over for dinner." She said as she went to the kitchen. "I was telling her about the tamale pie I made last night."

She didn't even notice that I was sulking, "I hope she gets fat!"

Olive started laughing, "why would you say that?"

"Your kitty was calling me for some catnip and then you invite her over. You two are going to start talking about work, and I will be in the bed long before she's gone."

"Like I've never woke you up?"

"It's not the same."

"How about a quickie?"

"Olive you insult me! My desire is long and strong. I don't want no quickie...." She smiled at me, "right now." She smiled at me like she knew better. I walked in the kitchen claiming I was thirsty. Ok, ok, so I bent her over the counter. I just don't like the whole idea behind quickies. My lovemaking is not quick.

Julia came over with her little almost unnoticeable belly. Spencer told her he wanted a blood test to be certain, and that he would be there for his child. I know he wanted to wash his hands from the whole thing and run, but Paula and Olivia were watching him for his response. If he ran out on her, Paula would've dropped him and he's made a lot of professional connections being on her arm. With one more year until his masters he needed all the connections he could make. And if he's delusional and thinks he could ever have a chance with my Olive Oil he has to be a stand-up guy. Julia wanted to be insulted that Spencer said he wanted a blood test. Olive talked her down and told her that getting it would work out for the best. I wonder if she wondered about the paternity of the baby secretly.

"Why would you leave? This summer isn't like last summer, you could stay." Julia said

"I have to see my family." Julia was emotionally attached to every conversation. I would look at Olive and then I'd go in my room. This girl looked like she was going to cry because I was leaving. My sister was sensitive when she was pregnant, but this girl cries about everything. She eats and cries, I look at Olive and then I retreat to my game room or our bedroom. Olive is always catering to her. I know she feels bad for her. Spencer should be dealing with this, he's the one who knocked her up…. we think.

This summer, I'm going home for six weeks, then I'm coming back. We won't be apart nearly as long, but it still feels like a lifetime. "Olivia you promised to be my partner in my Lamaze classes."

"What does that have to do with summer?"

"Classes start in August."

"August what? She's coming to Richmond with me for a week, then we're coming back together."

"It should be fine Jani, I'm coming out the first weekend of the month."

"That's when my class is." She started crying again. "I need you Livy!"

I looked at Olive and sucked my teeth. "We already bought our tickets, besides why would you reschedule with me for her. Tell her she better get it together."

"Livy!" She whined.

"Julia, how could you try to make me choose between you and Jani? That's not even right!"

"Livy, I don't have anyone else."

"Ask Spencer to go."

She cried harder, "you know he doesn't care about what happens to me or the baby. He told me he was wishing for a miscarriage all through my first trimester. He's so callous he could care less about anyone or anything."

"I told you he's been through a lot."

"I know he's been through a lot we talked about all that. We talked about a lot of stuff. I thought he kind of cared about me. At least more than this. I wasn't trying to get pregnant on purpose, and especially not like this. I always imagined my husband would be excited when I told him I was pregnant. That he would have a grateful response for all that I'm risking and putting my body through."

Olive rubbed her back, "I know Jewels. But you got to remember that Jani comes first in my life. You can't try to make me choose."

I couldn't take anymore of their tears and sympathy for each other. I got up and walked away.

****

I get off on watching her face as I take her there. She turns red and then it's like she tries to hold it back but I make her feel so good she can't control it. I used to listen to her body to know when to go, now when her body starts to tell me, it's important to me to watch her face. When you think about it, that moment when you cum is probably your ugliest moment. All my life I was teased about having big eyes, and ears that stuck out just a little. When I hit about fifteen I finally started growing into my features. When I watch the video, my awkward features are back in full affect. My eyes buck out mostly, fortunately this girl loves me enough not to have noticed or even care at that point. She says I stare now, and I don't care. The lights have to be on, and either she's facing a mirror or we're twisted up where I can see. I have to see what I'm doing to her, that according to her no one has done before. I grabbed her hair and pulled her head back, "I need to see my beautiful Olive! Daddy's going away for a few weeks. I need to see this." Olive sat up kissed me, and she pushed me backwards. See she rides when she's trying to assert herself over me. I love it when she tries, but she still can't handle me when I'm on my back. I hold on to her hips so I don't buck her into the ceiling. As she looked down at me her hair kept falling forward. I love it, but it annoys her. I grabbed her face and brought her up to kiss me while I hit her spot and rendering her motionless. Every time I do this she freezes up like she doesn't remember this part. "Purr for daddy baby!" Little miss Olive is rendered unresponsive as she frowns in the sweetest ecstasy that makes her walls grip me. I try to hold out, but she contracts all around me. I have one more round in me to completely seal the deal. I reach for another condom, and I'm out. I say a silent curse. I flush the one I'm wearing then I get back in the bed to take her right back to speechlessness before she notices that we're skin to skin. I go back in deep and long, Olive gasp, she tries to back away from me, but I won't let her. Her eyes are wide and I lay in on her spot until this one comes stronger than the last one. I kiss her, then I put my arms around her.

Once Olivia catches her breath her body became cold and angry. "What happened to your condom?"

"I ran out," I was drifting off to sleep.

"You didn't get more when I asked you to?"

"Did you feel the dick skin condom I was wearing? That should answer your question."

"This is not a game Ahjani, babies can and will happen."

"Did you get off the pill?"

"No."

"Then we have nothing to worry about. This is a dumb argument to have, especially right now."

"I don't want to get pregnant right now."

"And you won't."

"If you keep slacking off like this. Anything could happen."

Ok, she's working my nerves now, and undoing all the work I just put in for both of our peace of minds on our last night together. "Olivia! Calm down! My name is not Spencer and your name is not Julia. If we did end up pregnant I would take care of you!"

"Really? How? I pay most of the bills around here. I'm the breadwinner, there's no guarantee you're going to go pro. You haven't even acted like you're considering it, and it's going to be another three years at least before you're finished with school and in debt up to the ceiling."

I got out of the bed, "you're the one who wanted this fancy townhouse that is beyond my budget. Last year I paid ALL the bills while you tried to figure out what you wanted to do with yourself. Give you a little money and look how you act. The thought of having my baby takes you to the land of all evil, fine. Don't worry about it, I won't touch you again without a condom. The dragon lady in you comes out whenever you think about children anyways. Honestly, I don't think you really want to have any anyways." I knew my reference to her mother hurt her, but she hurt me too. Right now, I can't afford all this fancy excessive stuff. Even as the poor man's dentist I would be able to provide a decent living. Jason has been advising me on financial courses. Stuff he studied while in jail at the urging of his best friend. He said his best friend kept money on his books and when his cousin got locked up they studied together. He said that was all they really had time for in there was studying, planning, and studying some more. I wouldn't be poor, and my children would be taken care of.

Our argument went on for hours, neither one of us would let anything go. In the end I was moving my flight to a later time, packing my things and putting them in storage. I wasn't coming back to this townhouse, and now I was single.

Chapter 8

Olivia

Ahjani was mad, and this is the biggest argument that we've ever had. I ended up leaving and letting myself in at Paula's before the sun was up. I sent her a text and I told her I was going to be in my old room when she needed me. She replied ok, I cried my eyes out. When she came in my room she looked like she had been having sex all night too. She asked me if I was ok, and I shook my head no. Paula is the only mother figure I have, so I cried into her arms as I told her about the argument Ahjani and I had. She let me get it all out while she held me and rocked me gently like my grandmother used to do. In that moment I missed her so much! I wished she was still here, that Royal and my little brother weren't the only family members who honestly cared about me. She asked me if I wanted to hear the good or the bad first. I told her to give me the bad first. She got on my case about picking an argument after sex. She told me unless I was trying to drive the man away, you NEVER do that. She said that applied both ways. She said that's right up there with the rules of not waiting until you're in bed to argue. She said that is the quickest way to kill intimacy. A relationship without intimacy wasn't a relationship. Then she reminded me that Ahjani happily took care of both of us last year and he didn't demand that I get a job or even find and immediate direction for my life. She said that he has been nothing but patient with me, and he didn't want the expensive fancy townhouse, but because it was what I wanted we got it. She was gently going in so badly on me I wondered if there was an upside to any part of this. The good part was that I stood up for myself and I didn't allow the fact of possibly losing the love of my life to make me a weeping willow. I screamed when she said that, I asked her if she thought I could really lose him. Then she reminded me of how vicious I was in this argument unlike any other argument we've ever had. She told me to go home immediately and try to make up with him. She said I needed to apologize. When I tried to call his cellphone, I kept getting the operator who told me I had miss dialed or reached a number that was no longer in service. Ahjani's keys were on the table and all of his stuff, the little bit he had was gone. I told myself to stop panicking. I assumed that he went to the storage facility that we were at last year. When I got there they were just opening for the day, and they asked me if I wanted to open a unit. I raced to the airport, I was hoping to catch him in the line before the security checkpoint, but of course the airport would be efficient today and the line was barely there. I ran up to the ticket counter and I gave the guy a sob story about my grandmother having lung cancer (cause she did, she was a chain smoker and she couldn't kick the habit even for me.) and that I desperately needed to see her one last time. I doubt the guy heard a word I said, his eyes were glued to my V-neck T-shirt and the bounce of my cleavage as I pleaded with him for a ticket to go to my grandmother's gate. I blew the guy a kiss when he gave me the ticket then I ran back to the security checkpoint. Once I was through security, I searched the board for all flights to Oakland Airport. Ahjani only flies direct flights so that helped me narrow down where I was running to.

Ahjani

"Thank you Princess Fiona," I said taking the cup of tea she offered me.

"You are the last person I expected to be ringing my phone at all hours of the morning." She rubbed my leg as she sat next to me. "So you guys broke up?" She watched my face for an answer. I focused on my cup, I didn't want to answer. "It's ok Ahjani, what's said here stays here."

"We've discussed our plan, suddenly my plan isn't good enough. Suddenly she doesn't need me for anything further than being the dick when she needs some. I don't know if she became Thing 1 or Thing 2?"

"What is your plan?"

"It doesn't matter now."

"You know Gordon is going to try to go pro this year if he can manage instead of waiting until next year."
I blew air, "of course he is. I bet he's pissing off school just like Spencer did. The difference is that Omar doesn't come from a well off family where they can afford to pay his way through school when his dream of being the star of the NBA draft falls apart. Omar comes from a single parent family like I do. Opportunities like this only come along every so often for guys like us; Richmond California, single parent families. He makes it to the NBA then what? He's making money and he's spending money.

He'll end up broke thinking that the money will keep coming. If he doesn't get endorsement deals or shine on the court he will get cut. I'm going to make money no matter which way my life goes, and that money is going to work for me. I'm trying to stay level headed about this whole thing." The pain of Olivia stabbed me, I was quiet for a minute. I looked at the clock, it was thirty minutes before my original flight was supposed to leave. I planned to leave Fiona's in an hour, find a storage unit on the ground level where I could drive my car with all of my things in it in. Lock it up and come back for it for next school year. I chuckled, "now she can go to Lamaze class with Julia."

Fiona flinched, "Julia's pregnant?"

"You didn't know?"

"I haven't talked to her in ages. Whose baby is it?"

I shrugged, "it's Julia. Who knows."

"Spencer didn't tell me he was expecting a baby."

My lips curled up in disgust, "you see Spencer?"

She sucked her teeth, "not like that. He's on the track with us most times. Sometimes we run together. How loose do you think I am?"

I eyed her, "I don't know. You let Omar in."

"It was only one time, and I was drunk. It shouldn't have happened."

I gave her a look, "only one time?"

She laughed, "yes! He was no good! Besides, he met someone shortly after that and they've been dating ever since. Not that he's the faithful type, but I'm not a take your man type either. I guess that's why it hurt when you got with Olivia. I didn't take you seriously when you were talking about needing love in your life. I thought you were trying to run game on me. You already had me addicted to the D, I couldn't risk falling in love with you too."

"What's wrong with falling in love with me?"

"If I were Olivia I'd do whatever you wanted me to do. If you wanted me to have ten of your babies I would. I know what sex with you is like, I can only imagine what making love with you is like. The thought of it scares me."

"That's why you ran from me?"

She shook her head yes, "and the fact that you said you like curvy women. You would've had me fat, happy and satisfied. Who needs that kind of completeness in their lives? I would've been too happy and unable to hold on to my drive for corporate America."

I shook my head, "you have issues."

"I cried the morning after I slept with Gordon. On top of the fact that he wasn't any good. I knew that put the nail in the coffin for you and I. I'm sorry."

"Thank you for knowing."

She exhaled like she wished I would've said she had it all wrong or something. "Yeah, can I at least be stuck in the friends zone?"

"We are friends Princess Fiona."

She made breakfast then she followed me to the storage facility I used last year. They had one unit like the one I needed available. I locked up my things then Fiona and I slowly went to the airport. Before we got to my terminal we stopped at the light so that pedestrians could pass. I spotted Olivia balling her eyes out as she walked towards the garage, if my ears weren't on the receiving end of every mean and hurtful thing she said I might've felt bad for her. I might've went to her, but since she didn't think twice about the things that came out of her mouth that stained my ears and would never leave my memory, I let her go. Fiona didn't see her, I hugged my friend and I thanked her for everything. Then I went inside the airport and eventually boarded my plane like I was supposed to.

Olivia

"Our mother wanted me to give you this number the next time I talked to you but I kept forgetting."

"I don't want her number." I protested.

"It's not hers, I don't know who's number it is."

It's was a 510 area code so it was someone in the Bay. I dialed the number, as soon as I heard the voice on the end I hung up. I made a disgusted face. When my little brother asked who it was, I told him it was my sperm donor. I couldn't even bring myself to say father. When the phone rang, I cursed the person who invented Call Return and Caller ID. "Dudley residence,' my little brother said as he answered the phone. Then he handed the phone to me.

"Olivia, this is your father. Why did you hang up in my face?"

"Because I realized it was you. What do you want?"

"I want a do over, I realize that I was an absentee father, and I want to make that up to you."

"How do you think that's even possible?"

"For starters I'd like to cover your student loans. I should've offered to cover everything when you graduated."

"Well I guess if you actually cared to come to my graduation you could've covered that then."

He ignored my comment, "I want to come out and visit you out in Georgia. You know come, spend some time getting to know you, and you I."

"Why would I want to get to know you?"

"Because knowing me will answer questions for you about who you are."

"I already know that I've inherited the capability to hurt people with my words from you."

He ignored me again, "when can I come out?"

"I barely got out here today. Let me think about it. Maybe you can come in a week or two." I couldn't believe I said that.

"A week or two? Oh! Um! How about I come in a couple of months. Let you get settled back into the school habits."

"I doubt I will have time, my job demands most of my free time."

"Oh you can quit your job. I'll cover your expenses." I looked at the phone, this was awfully generous for the man who hated paying child support. "Besides more free time will give you more time to focus on your relationship."

A heat wave flashed over my body. "What do you know about my relationship?"

"Your mother told me."

"You speak to my mom?"

"All the time, we met for drinks and a game was on. When I told her how much I like the young man on the screen during a college game. She excitedly told me that she's met him and that you two were dating."

I hung up the phone, I told my little brother to tell that man that he has no daughter when he called back.

****

"Olivia? Honey? What are you doing here?" Aquilla asked

85

"I was hoping to catch Ahjani home."

"He's not here, he went back to school already." She watched my eyes, "you want to come in? Audra is making dinner."

"No, I don't want to intrude."

"Nonsense, get in here." She moved so I could come inside. "Ahjani's been gone for two weeks now."

"Does he hate me?"

"He's pretty hurt, he didn't go into a lot of details. I'm just the mom."

"I was freaking out, I didn't mean to hurt him."

"I don't know the details, and I don't want to know. All I want to know is when you wear him down and you two get back together."

After dinner I helped Audra clean the dishes. She bumped me and smiled, She said with Ahjanae room mating with their cousin, she was on duty to be the ears to hear Ahjani out. I asked her if he was done with me. He had been home two weeks before I left to come out here, and he didn't try to call me or come by. "Olivia, I like you. No, we all like you. So I'm going to tell you the truth. Never do this again! You can't take back your words once they escape your lips or the damage those words permanently cause. All you can do is throw yourself on the mercy of the court." She smiled, "my big brother is a bit of a romantic. Go to him! Don't give up on him! He still loves you, he's just hurting."

"Georgia is a pretty big state, I don't know where to find him. I couldn't even find him at the airport."

"But you know what school he goes to, and you know what team he's playing for. Go!"

Ahjani

Swish! Swish! Swish! I was focused! Surprisingly as much as I like to have sex, the urgency to have it wasn't there. I remember when I couldn't go days, and here it is three months later and I'm not concerned. I've hung out a few times with the Princess, but she knows I'm not interested. I don't know how, but something inside of me changed when I ran into Nellie's parents one day. Mr. Parker was his normal reserved self, but Mrs. Parker was so happy to see me. She gave me a hug before her husband could object to it. When I asked how Nellie was doing, he quickly replied that she was fine, and then he told his wife they had to go.

The look she gave him for whatever reason said to me that Nellie would've been happy to hear from me. Everything in me changed. My ache for Olivia lessened a lot. I drove by their old house and sure enough they still live there. All of my memories of Nellie flooded my brain. She was the one that I learned everything with, my first real girlfriend, my first love, and my first heartbreak. I didn't know what I would do if I saw her..... WHO AM I KIDDING! If she would've walked out of that house, all sense of right and wrong would've gone out the window. I wouldn't care if she was supposed to have a man, or if I was supposed to be with someone. She is the one who got away! That's who I want, and that's who I'm going to prepare myself for. I'm not worried about Olivia! She can cut all her hair off again for as much as I care. Her flip out was, and is, system overload for me. "Lubbock!" Douglas said giving me a high five. "Excellent practice! This season is going to be better than the last."

"That's what I'm working towards."

As if it was possible, your woman has gotten finer!"

I cut my eyes at him as I mocked him, "as if it was possible."

"She was standing in the wind for you, waiting for you to catch a glimpse of her in all of her dramatics. I don't know how you never looked. Coach said you are focused."

I took a deep breath that means she's out there. I didn't want to deal with her just yet. Suddenly my pace became very slow. I showered slowly, lather, scrub, rinse, and repeat. There wasn't a crevice that wasn't fresh on my body. You could eat off these balls. I was one of the last people out of the locker room. Olivia was patiently waiting. DANG IT SHE DOES LOOK GOOD! I had no visible reaction to her. She walked up to me and started apologizing immediately. I felt like it was only right to apologize for not discussing our choices with her before I went back in. More than likely in the heat of the moment she would've had the same resolve as I did, but since I didn't discuss it with her I was just as responsible for the cause of the argument as she was. However, I didn't go in on her like she went in on me. So I stood there looking at her as she apologized for a long time. As long as I stood there not speaking she kept apologizing. I was tired and I wanted to go home. I told her to give me her number and I'd call her. She started to ask me if I deleted her number, but that was a dumb question. I wouldn't have asked for it if I had it.

Chapter 9

Olivia

It took Ahjani forever to call me. At one point I was devastated that he wasn't actually going to call. When he finally called I was so relieved that I told myself to be on best behavior, which didn't last long. We ended up arguing again when he called. It was nothing like our last argument of course, but this wasn't the Olivia and Ahjani interaction that I was used to. He told me that he felt like the real me came out that night, and I had been hiding who I was all this time. I kept arguing that I freaked out and the person he argued with was a very scared and frightened me. When I felt like he only called me to tell me he didn't want to be with me I lost it. I cried hard! It felt like my heart was ripping in my chest right at that moment. Ahjani hung up on me and I thought that was it for us. I laid on the floor and cried. I was still crying twenty minutes later when he was at my door. He told me to put on shoes and then he took me to an all-night coffee shop where I tried to keep my tears in check. He watched my face as I cried, then he told me I was using my tears against him. I apologized and tried to pull it back. I wanted him to want me and love me like he did before. I wanted the Ahjani back who liked to watch the video of us together. The one who was in love with me. The guy in front of me right now is very guarded and analytical. I couldn't help it, I cried when he told me he still loved me, but I hurt him really badly when I said all those mean and hurtful things. He didn't want to hear me apologize for the millionth time. He said we needed to back up and start over, which I agreed to. However, now it's been months and he hasn't tried to sleep with me. He nicely turns me down and he's not interested. He won't move back in with me, and he has his own place about ten miles away from me. I thought maybe he's cheating on me with someone else at the very least Fiona. But he's not, he used to have to have me. Now he doesn't. He'll kiss me, and we'll make out. But he won't go in. I know I messed up but this torture is beyond all comprehension.

Ahjani

Damn! I am surprising myself with my reaction to all of this. I know I still love her, I know I still want her. However, every time we start going in that direction something about the last time we were together flashes in my mind and I can't do it. Blue balls have become a normal way of life for me. I needed to talk to someone, so I broke down and called my teammate Baker. He's in a committed relationship and has been for almost as long as Olivia and I have been together. We talked around relationships and he said in so many words that we hadn't healed from the incident yet. We needed to heal.

****

At warm-up he kept looking at me as usual. Nothing about that idiot has changed in all these years. Omar is still in my shadow and a non-threat to me. Omar told me he was going to whoop me in his house. I said nothing, there was no point in arguing with him. My proof would be in the final score. I scanned the crowd out here. What a difference a state made. This school was more diverse in its attendees, there were a few white folks at my school, and more Fiona's than white, but mostly black folks. Fiona could probably pass for Sicilian but a lot of times she said people asked her if she was of Latin descent. I don't exactly know what her background consists of either, she refers to herself as a black woman, and I don't question it. It doesn't matter, not to me anyways. There were a lot of Fiona's at this school though. It looked like Omar was looking for someone in the stands, which had him, more distracted than he needed to be. As usual we beat ASU. I went to the locker room. I knew he was probably going to throw some sort of tantrum when I came out the locker room. I was going to throw my victory in his face and then get on my bus back to the hotel. "Omar I told you, you could never beat...." It felt like I was looking at a mirage. "NELLIE?" I blinked a couple times to make sure my eyes weren't playing tricks on me.

"Hi," she said like she was embarrassed.

I stumbled backwards, "Nellie! You disappeared! I...."

"I know, I'm sorry. There was a lot going on back then."

Omar put his arm around Nellie with a big smile. "How do you know my girlfriend?"

I heard him wrong right? Did he just say, "girlfriend? This is wrong on so many levels!"

"Wrong?" Omar said

"Nellie is my ex."

"Puppy love though. You weren't serious about anyone until Olivia." Omar said like he was delivering facts about my life to me.

I shook my head no, "I was serious about her. She disappeared. Where did you go?

"My father made me come to his office after school. They kept me so busy," she looked me in my eyes like she does in my dreams. "I couldn't hurt you like that." Then she looked at the ground before Omar caught the love in her eyes for me.

"You guys were together together?" His whole little dumb plan backfired. I bet he thought he was going to show off his girl toy and I was supposed to feel like he still won even though he lost. Instead you could see the sexual tension in the air. "Yes!" We said in unison.

As Omar stood there asking questions it was clear as day that he regretted his choice to unite us. He really regretted it once he realized that not only did Nellie and I have unfinished business, but she and Kendra used to be close at one point. I stared at Nellie taking everything about her in, a feeling I hadn't felt in a long time washed over me. It was desire! I could feel and see her desire for me, and I knew she was picking up on my vibe. "You missed your bus, you need a ride?"

My heart started pounding, she wasn't going to make me chase her. She needed me too. "Yes." Then I looked at Omar. "This is what you get for trying to be a show off!" Then I laughed.

Nellie moved her backpack to the back seat of her car, then I got in. Omar was acting like the punk he is moving around too much in the front. I took her notebook out of her backpack I wrote my room number on the first page. When we got to my hotel I thanked her for the ride, and then I forced myself to get up and to go inside. I had nervous energy. I didn't care what time she came to me, as long as she came to me. If she couldn't get away I could call a cab and come to where she is. Everything inside of me was on fire and I had to see her. I called Olivia to get our normal call out of the way. I told her we won, she sounded a little distracted. I asked her what was going on, and she said she was at Julia's and she was in the early part of labor. That was not something I wanted to think about in this moment. We talked for a few minutes and then she had to go as I heard Julia moaning in pain in the background. I paced the floor for a few minutes wondering if Omar found a way to keep her hostage. I was willing to miss my flight and forgo all else to pay for my own ticket home just to stay until I could have alone time with Nellie. I was at a full erection when she knocked at the door. I opened the door and snatch her in. Her hair, her perfume, everything was exactly the way I remembered it. My hands were all through her hair, and all over her body. We moved to the bed, to the chair, to the counter for the sink. This kitty was different, she purred for daddy right away and rapid fire. This little kitty was a slave to my catnip, BUT this kitty. This kitty is the only kitty to turn me out just like I turned it out. Daddy missed this kitty so much! No fear of hurting her, she took me to that place of putting my ALL in. I wished I had a camera, cause I wanted to see this on repeat all day every day. I was home, this was my future.

I put her number in my phone, and mine in hers. I told her I always come home even if it was only briefly every summer. She said she had to go home or else her little sister would have a heart attack. I told her I could make it through the rest of this year as long as I knew that this summer I would see her again. I wasn't letting go this time.

Olivia

"Congratulations Ms. Blaze, it's a boy." The doctor said as he placed the baby on Julia's chest. He was changing colors as he cried the newborn congested cry.

Julia touched him and kissed him as she said hello to him. All the why me's, and her life was over, complaints melted away. Julia was in love with her little man. "Hello Julian, it's nice to meet you." She said to the baby.

They took the baby from her to clean him up, I told Julia he was beautiful. She thanked me, she was at peace suddenly. They wrapped him up and passed him to me. He responded to my voice, which was amazing to see. I took pictures of us. I gave the baby back to Julia and then I went out to the waiting room. Spencer was in the waiting room pacing while Paula nodded off in her seat. I cleared my throat to get their attention. "Julian is here."

"I have a son?" Spencer smiled widely.

"Yes you do."

"Can I go in? I want to see him."

"Of course you can."

Spencer turned to Paula, "we'll be right back." Then he followed me out of the waiting room. "I'm happy we got the DNA testing out of the way before this moment. I HAVE A SON!" He smiled so big.

"Yes you do, and you better remember this moment every time you feel like things are getting too difficult. You can play dumb all you want, but Julia loves you. What woman goes through all of this for someone she doesn't care for? Be good to my friend, be good to your son."

Spencer looked at me like he was amazed. Then he grabbed me and kissed me. He caught me completely off guard, and his kiss sent electricity up my leg. "You are amazing." Then he released me and walked in the room.

I stood there feeling stuck. What was that? I touched my lips to try to understand if that was real. My stomach was fluttering and and and and...... HOW WRONG IS THAT? My best friend just gave birth to their child, while he waited in the waiting room with his girlfriend who's my boss. I wanted Spencer to come back out here so I could punch him. How dare he make me feel anything for him. I took a few pictures of the three of them together. Then I went back to the waiting room with Paula. She patted the seat next to me while she grinned at me. "What did he do?"

HOW DID SHE KNOW? I was scared she was going to be mad at me. "I was giving him a lecture about being good to his son and he kissed me."

She forced a chuckle as she rubbed my hands to calm my nerves. "That boy has been in love with you for some time now."

"ME?"

"Yep, you're the only one who acts like you don't know it."

"But, I'm in love with Ahjani."

"I know, how's the young love working out these days. You don't seem very happy anymore."

Tears poured out of my eyes, "he doesn't love me anymore. The last time we made love was right before our argument. Every time we've gotten close to doing it he fizzles out. His eyes don't hold that same love for me anymore. Do you think he could love me and not have sex with me?"

"I remember what young love feels like. Either you two will work it out or you will move on. Your world will not stop turning Livy. Stop waiting for him to forgive you. You apologized and that part of your life is over, you will never make that same mistake twice will you?"

"NEVER!" I cried.

"Do you think he's cheating on you?"

"I wish, that would be somehow easier to deal with than this. I've followed him around and popped up as randomly as I could. He's not cheating, he's just turned off."

"You have to turn him back on. How did you get him the first time?"

"I don't know, by being me and being willing to love him."

"Did you sleep with him right away?"

"No, he waited months for me."

"He always came to you for sex?"

"No, but I didn't have to work for it."

She smiled, "those two are going to be locked up in baby land for the next however long. I just hope she doesn't get pregnant within the first six weeks."

"You think she's going to sleep with him after all of this?"

"PLEASE! If she told you that they ever stopped having sex she lied to you. That's her baby's daddy now. She's always going to be open to him. That's his firstborn and it's a son. Those two may not technically get together, but they're now bonded for life." She exhaled, "any who, we can use that time to focus on you."

"Spencer is still your boyfriend?"

She rubbed my hand. "Yes, but you're not going to end up alone like me. I don't have the space in my heart to let someone in. I need a man, preferably a young man." She winked at me, "only for certain things. I'm too bitter to ever let a man truly in my heart. I've been hurt too many times. I don't want you to end up like me so I'm going to help you. Spencer's not going to say or do anything for a while, he's in love with his son. It's up to you if you allow your curiosity for him to take over." I gasped like I was going to object. "Don't you dare twist your mouth to deny it, you're talking to me. People are always going to tell you that curiosity killed the cat, but few people even know that satisfaction brought him back. Sometimes we have to act on our curiosities. Would I encourage you to do it? No, cause you will chip away at yourself for allowing it."

"Seduction huh?"

"Yes, when does he come back?"

"Today."

"Oh well we don't have much time. Wipe that sleep out of your eyes, class is in session."

Ahjani

I was lost in my thoughts the entire plane ride. I kept smelling my fingers, they were covered in Nellie. I almost vowed to never wash my hands again, but that was just nasty. Fortunately her smell lingered above my shower, it was barely there but it was there. I looked out the window at the clouds, then I remembered my angry bird. I didn't feel guilty until just now. I tried to justify my actions by stating that we were in a bad place. I had to be honest with myself, even if Olivia and I were happy like we were before, I still would be sitting on this plane feeling this same way. There was no way I was going to pass up a night with Nellie for anyone!

On my way home Olivia called, she asked if she could come over for dinner tomorrow. That was fine. Meanwhile I daydreamed and dreamed at night about my night with Nellie. It was just what I needed to feel like my old self again. Even though it was complicated my first love still loves me too.

I opened the door and Olivia had quite a few grocery bags in her hands and she was bundled up to protect herself from the winter cold outside. I took her bags and spread them out on the counter. I asked her if anything need to go in the freezer and she said no. She asked me to open the red wine to let it breathe while she went to the bathroom. I did as I was told. Her hair and makeup were done up really pretty and so I told her she looked nice. She thanked me, then she asked me to put on music while we prepared dinner. My stereo was in my bedroom I asked her what she wanted to hear, she said anything R&B. I was fidgeting with the CD rotation to make sure a lot of our old school classics played. The smells of the kitchen were filling the house with the aroma of a woman creating a mantrap. I smiled to myself. When I walked back out of the bedroom my mouth dropped open. Olivia had stripped down to her matching pink and black bra and panties set. She had on high heels, and a pink and white apron that said kiss the cook. She brought me a glass of red and she told me to have a seat. She asked me how my flight was. I told her I thought about her as I looked out at the clouds. She smiled and said angry birds. Then she told me about her conversation with her father this summer. She started chopping the vegetables harder as she recalled the whole thing to me. Chopping harder made everything that was supposed to move jiggle. She had my complete attention. I told her that at graduation I was going to enter the draft. If I didn't get picked up then that was that. If I did get picked up I was still going to keep dentistry in my plans because nothing was guaranteed. She looked at me as she placed my plate in front of me and repeated that nothing was guaranteed. She used my fork to put a forkful in my mouth as she said it again. Everything was delicious. When I finished she took my plate away, she took off her apron, then she sat on the counter in front of me. She opened her legs so I could smell her desire. Then she proceeded to talk to me like she wasn't swimming in her panties. I tried to focus on her words, but it was like her kitty was calling me. As I slid my fingers under her panties she looked me in my eyes and said that was always guaranteed. Then she gave me a peck on the lips and then she got off the counter. She walked away from me like I wasn't just touching her. Something that normally renders her speechless. She told me she brought movies, she held up my options as if I wasn't going to pick Love Jones. I went in my room, took off my shirt and pants, then I put condoms under the pillow on the couch just in case we got that far while she was in the bathroom. I laid on the couch in my briefs and she sat on my recliner with her legs open as she watched the movie. I joked with her asking her why she made me wait so long when people in the movies do it right away. She laughed and said this is real life and she needed me to know she didn't pass herself around like she didn't value herself. She bounced her feet as she giggled and I told myself to stop looking. Then I asked her why she was all the way over there. I told her we always watch movies laying down together on the couch. As soon as she laid next to me my hand went in for her wetness. She was so hard up I made her purr to the rhythm of my fingers. So much for the movie, it was on.

Daddy had this kitty purring all over my living room, and just like that we were back in the game.

Chapter 10

Olivia

I had the biggest bouquet of flowers I could afford, and a cute little teddy bear sent to Paula. It said,

Dear Mommy Paula,

Thank you for taking the time to help me get my man back. I owe you my sanity!

Love,
Liv

Even though she'd never own up to it. I KNOW she likes those kinds of sentimental gestures. I think that's why we get along so well. We have that feature in common.

Although we're back to the loving, something's different. Technically everything is the same, he still blows my mind, and the sex is still amazing. If I had to put my finger on it. YES! That's what it is. He used to constantly reassure me that he loved me and no one could mean more to him than me. Now he says I love you too. Meaning I'm always saying it first. Sometimes it's like he didn't think to say it until I said it, and it's like... Oh yea, I love you too.

Sometimes I wonder if he saw someone while we were apart. He says no, and now even more so now he barely looks at Fiona like she exist. If I didn't think they were just friends before, I'm convinced of it now. She seems hurt by his disregard of her as well. Sometimes he'll be looking at me and then he looks right through me. When I warned him that I was going to get my normal healthy ends trim he barely reacted. Before he used to want to know how much hair I was cutting off. He'd tell me not to let the stylist get scissor happy in my hair. When I'd come home his hands would be all in it. Now...... So this time I told the Stylist to take and extra two inches off cause this hair was getting way too long. She was shocked but she did as she was told. Ahjani only shrugged when he pointed out that I cut my hair. At least he noticed, but he didn't seem to care.

****

"Jules! You're getting heavy! I don't know if I can be carrying you around." As if he understood what I was saying he smiled at me. He gets too excited whenever I come around. Spencer seems to find his way around whenever I'm holding the baby too. You know babies especially breast fed babies have a tendency to be obsessed with breast. Jules is no exception. He tries to put his hand down my shirt. When he's ready to eat he nuzzles his head in your breast. Spencer likes to watch cause he knows eventually it's going to happen. Since we don't live together anymore, and Ahjani refuses to consider the idea for now, Julia asks if we're still together. She never sees us together anymore. I mostly go over his place when he's home. I travel a lot too these days. If it's not for my personally requested gig, then it's to work with Paula on her gigs and seminars. She tells me all the time to model myself after her, and to do whatever she's done. One time I got annoyed because someone, ok it was Julia but still. She copied my concept for a photo-shoot down to the actual location. Paula asked me why that would bother me. Someone liked what I did so much that they wanted to make it their own. She told me that was flattery. I told her flattery and her spin on it was fine. My problem was, when persons like Julia would see what I've done, and sit back as if they could do it better. That was what I was really upset about. She told me I would often be imitated, but never would I be duplicated. There was only one me, and as long as I was confident in my work why did it matter what other people did? I knew she was right, and I told her it was going to take some time for me to mature to her level. Especially if someone's duplication got them more acclaim than my original masterpiece. She told me it didn't matter. One day I would get there. "Livy loves the baby." I gave him a kiss.

Spencer watched us, "when are you going to have your own?"

"The plan is to do it after we've been married a few years."

"When are the nuptials supposed to take place?"

"Once he's done with school."

He smiled, "you making sure he acquires that debt prior to your marriage so you're not accountable for it. That's smart."

I looked at Spencer, "when do you approach anything with heart? Marriage is a beautiful union of souls. Not some business idea that you approach like a company merger."

"You couldn't handle it, so....."

I switched hips to bounce the baby, "stop talking. Please!"

"This may be my only chance." He tilted his head, "Lubbock doesn't even see you anymore. It's clear as day his heart is taken. I see you, I want you. I'd give you everything I have and I'd bust my butt to get the rest. I love you Olivia!"

I could feel my pores open on my head. I was about to start sweating. "Stop it!" I looked at the baby.

"The only reason Julia let me in, in the first place is because I told her I was in love with you."

"ALL THE WAY BACK THEN?" I didn't mean to react, but that was two years ago.

"Yes, some friend huh. Now I'm supposed to be the bad guy when she did all this. I mean I played my part, but she knows this was never about her or for her. Everything I've done for her was for you. Lubbock doesn't even care anymore."

"Stop it! You were rebounding from Courtney. As soon as you think about it, you'll know it's true." The baby's lip started shaking cause he was watching my face. "Oh Jules! It's ok!" I put on a fake smile.

Spencer walked up on me and grabbed my face, he knew I couldn't run or fight with the baby in my arms. He kissed me deeply and passionately, there was that electricity again. I found myself giving in to the kiss, I backed away from him. He took the baby from me then he went out to Julia's desk. I locked my office door then I sat at my desk trying to get my bearings about myself. When I couldn't focus I called Paula from my cell in tears as I rushed past Spencer and out the door. All I said was hello and she told her team she needed fifteen minutes. I could tell when she was somewhere quiet. I tearfully told her everything. She chuckled when she said she would tell him to stop attacking me. I asked her if she told Spencer anything I told her. She said he was a good lay, but he was never that good where she'd lose her mind and flap her gums. I was kind of wishing that she was the leak, and that it wasn't obvious to the world that things had changed between Ahjani and I.

Ahjani

"You gotta stop with the gifts they're getting me in trouble." Nellie said although I could hear her smile and gratitude through the phone.

"Tell Omar to come see me if he has a problem with them."

"You know he's not going to do that."

I laughed, "exactly."

"How's Olivia?"

I exhaled, "why do you always do that?"

"Do what?"

"Mention her."

"Because that's who you're in love with."

"She's not you."

She smiled, "and who am I?"

"My first love!"

"The look on your face the first time I let you in was priceless." She smiled

"You taught me how to have sex like a champion."

"No I didn't, I simply became your practice to the greatness you are today. Marquez is a lot like you in a lot of ways."

Irritation! Is she really mentioning some other fool while she's talking to me? "There's only one Ahjani."

"Yes, but I'm talking about the way you always touched me. There was so much love in every touch. I'm sure you touch Olivia like that, Marquez does too."

"I wish I could touch you right now."

"Oh yeah?" Her voice smiled.

"Yep, I'd smack the heck out of you and tell you to stop talking about other people during our time."

We both laughed, "Ahjani you are so intense. I need you to relax. Your tension makes me tense, and then we're both stressed out for nothing."

"I'm trying to pull it back, but suddenly here you are after so many years without one single word. For years I've been dreaming about you, fantasizing even. Then here you are."

I could hear her smile through the phone, "you always make me feel special. The timing for this is so off. You've always been this wonderful guy. I won't let you turn that off for me. Be good to Olivia."

"That's kind of hard to do now that I realize that all I've wanted and needed over these years has been you. No one compares to you. When I gave my heart to you I never got it back."

"So it's kind of like your heart is already taken?"

"Yes, exactly."

She was quiet for a minute, "Ahjani so much has happened. As selfish as I am, I can love the fact that you're putting me on a pedestal. But I know what it's like to love someone who's in love with someone else and how no matter what you do they don't appreciate you. Don't be like that, it'll taint the way I see you. Be good to Olivia, do you love her?"

"Yes," I said in defeat.

"Don't lose her, be good to her."

"I wish you were here right now."

"Oh yeah, what would you do to me if I was there?"

"I'd grab you by the hair and make you kiss me."

I could hear her smile. "Oh yeah, then what?"

"As I kissed you, I'd put my hand down your shirt."

Even our phone sex was great! I didn't talk to her for a while.

****

"Our next honoree is Ahjani Lubbock!" The presenter said.

Everyone applauded me, I hugged my momma, Olivia, and my Auntie Kharee. Jason and I shook hands. They flew out for this dinner and to be here when I was presented with my award. I went up to the podium and then I looked back at my table. Olivia looked really pretty and she was excited and so happy for me. I gave my little thank you speech. My thank you to my momma for being a hard working single mother and doing the best she could with all of us. I thanked my Auntie Kharee for always being there for me and for us, and for not giving up on love and life and marrying the guy who's completed our family. I thanked Jason for showing me how to be a man. I told him that he filled the void that was left by the death of my stepfather. I debated on whether I would mention Olivia. At first I wasn't going to mention her at all. Then when I came up with the idea to have all the parental units stay at Olivia's place and have her stay with me. At first I didn't think I would like it, and I was going to have to tolerate her presence. However, I forgot how much fun it is to be with Olivia.

For the first time since we got back together I called her Olive, you would have thought I proposed to her. She was all over me. After a few days of it I remembered the love I used to have. I thanked Little Miss Olive Oil for always being there for me no matter what. Olivia was so touched that I mentioned her; I don't think she thought I was going to. I danced with my momma and then I danced with Olivia. It was a nice night. The next day Olivia had to work and so I took everyone sightseeing. My momma wanted to see where Olivia worked so we decided to pop up at her job. When we walked in the door Spencer was in Olivia's office standing too close to her while she held the baby. Jason frowned immediately at the scene. Julia came out the bathroom, she slowed down as she looked from one person to person. She looked in the direction of Jason and I's frown and then she said hi to me. I kept walking, I marched straight into the office. Olivia jumped really hard when I walked in. Spencer didn't move or look concerned. "What's going on?" Olivia asked nervously, "why are both of you mugging?"

"Who's baby?" Jason asked.

"My best friend Julia, this is Julian."

"And he is?"

"Nicholas Spencer, and you are?"

"Why are you all in her personal space?"

I looked at Jason, "he got a little crush on Olivia. I guess he's resorted to using the baby to get close to her."

"What? Ahjani, the baby is teething and we were looking at his gums." Olivia gave the baby back to Spencer. "Are we still on for dinner?" She was trying to change the subject.

Spencer walked out the room holding the baby and smirking at me. I hadn't thought about him pushing up on her. Now that she can afford it, her clothes are a lot better and nicely put together. I'm so quick to take them off; I hadn't really paid attention to her when she had them on. I know Spencer wants my girl; it's all over him no matter how dumb Olivia tries to play to that fact. "Come here." Olivia was hesitant but she did as she was told. I kissed her unlike I had kissed her in a long time. Jason walked out in the direction that Spencer went in, closing the door behind him. My mind had shifted gears so much; her love for me was all over the returned passion in her kiss. How did I forget about my Olive Oil? "Yes, we're still on for dinner tonight."

Her eyes were all dreamy, "Ahjani. You know I love you right?"

"You better," I smacked her butt. "He's using the baby to be in your space. You see that don't you?"

"His hands are full with Julia and Paula, I love you."

Chapter 11

Olivia

Paula and I took swallows of our glasses of wine. We were sitting in her hot tub relaxing.

Paula hates working with animals and children. And yesterday was nothing but that. I had a ball though, the kids were cute and the animals were professional. Paula couldn't get out of there fast enough when we were done. I conversed with the client a little and they were all smiles and pleased with what they saw thus far. Paula called me an hour later and she told me to come to her house in the morning instead of going into the office. She told me to bring my bikini.

Ahjani came over last night with dinner while I went over our pictures. He chose a favorite photo for each. He asked why Julian wasn't included in the shoot. I told him he was too little. I tried to change the subject cause conversations about the baby turned into interrogations about Spencer. I never told him about the times Spencer has spoken against him. I will never tell him about the kisses. I will say that he has stepped up a lot more since that day he popped up and saw Spencer here. He drops by the studio now, and he pops up at my place or more openly invites me over. He still seems torn about something though.

"I'm so happy yesterday is now yesterday. Since you thrive in that environment you can take all those gigs. I don't care how much they're paying, I'm over it."

"When you say stuff like that I wonder how you're going to be with Jules."

She huffed, she took another sip on her glass. "Spencer is nearing his expiration date. Pretty soon the only time I'll see or deal with him will be through Julia. Let's face it, that won't last too long once Spencer takes on his new role in his daddy's company. He graduates this summer and then it's bye bye beefcake. He was fun while he lasted." Then she looked at me, "what are you going to do?"

I let my eyes bounce around, "do?"

"Come on Liv you're talking to me. You have to know that if Spencer's leaving he's going to try to take you with him. He's in love with you."

"In love with me, sleeping with you and Julia."

"Please! Sex is just sex, I'm a good connection for him. And he was a nice toy for me. No pretenses or forced feelings. I don't understand why you've been so nice and forgiving with Julia."

"She's been through a lot, and she loves Spencer."

"That's her problem not yours. Why would she throw herself at someone who's hung up on you? She's going to spend her life competing. She messed up by getting pregnant. I don't trust her."

"So why did you hire her?"

"I needed an assistant." She shrugged, "shoot me."

I looked at the bubbles in the water, "summer's coming. It seems like Ahjani is excited about something or more like someone. Nothing is the same."

"Young love teaches you what to do and what not to in the future. You stand your ground and fight for Ahjani, but he has to want you too. Otherwise what are you fighting for?"

"Do you think he still loves me?"

"Yes, but he's distracted."

"Isn't that scandalous to get with a friend of your boyfriend? Not that I'm considering it."

"Oh of course not, you'd never consider something like that." She smiled as she took another drink. "Yes it is scandalous. But who cares? If in the end, the two of you are willing to rise above it, who cares. You have to do what's right for you. There's a part of you that cares about Spencer too. Otherwise you would've told Ahjani about him."

"I'm in love with Ahjani. I want to be with him even if it meant I worked to support us and he stayed home all day."

"Whoa! Whoa! Whoa! Let's not get ridiculous! Even if he's only flipping burgers your man has to work. Don't even put that nonsense out there." We laughed. "In all seriousness young love doesn't last. The impression does, you two are so young and you're still figuring out who you are. I want you two to make it, but the crumble of your relationship is typical."

"Are you purposely trying to steer me towards Spencer?"

She smiled, "I don't like Julia! A part of me wants her nose rubbed in everything."

I guess I'm the only person who feels sorry for Julia. I know she loves Spencer even if no one else sees it. We had massages and food catered in. We went over the pictures, photo shopped them to perfection. Then we sent our invoice for our services with one watermarked picture.

I've been saving my money instead of spending it like I did pre-life-altering-argument-of-words-without-filter. I figure this money will only help Ahjani and I while he's in dental school. Paula said it doesn't matter where I move as long as I'm willing to travel I'd still be employed with her. I sat there thinking about Ahjani. The guy from back home got picked up in the draft. Previously Ahjani was kind of passive about the NBA like it was a pipe dream or something. Now he holds his breath and says whatever happens happens.

As I walked in the door most of Ahjani's place was packed up. I didn't want him to go. "You could stay with me for the summer."

"Olivia, I need to go home. Weird stuff has been happening. I need to check in."

"You seem so happy to be getting away." I took a deep breath. "When can we talk?"

Ahjani stared at me for a minute. He didn't look irritated or angry, but that definitely wasn't a happy expression on his face. "Now," he put everything down and then he sat on the couch.

I wanted to back out, I screamed internally. "Ok," I cleared my throat. "What happened to us?" He tilted his head at me. "You stopped loving me?"

"Honestly, you know you turned me off. We've been rebounding from that."

"Ahjani, I wasn't the only person who was wrong that night." I looked at the floor.

"One selfish act doesn't outweigh another. I'll give you that. Your mouth was vicious, and you fought dirty. I try to overlook it, but the nastiness you showed me that night I never want to experience that again. Females who talk like that are the ones who get choked out by lesser men."

"Do you still love me?"

My heart pounded while ten of the longest seconds passed. "Yes, however I think we should try the summer apart."

Tears dripped out of my eyes as I shook my head. "You don't love me." He looked at me irritated. "When you loved me you couldn't stand to be away from me. When you loved me you couldn't bare the thought of someone else with me. Now.... Now this? This is not fair Ahjani, I messed up. I made a mistake, you're holding the past against me. It's not fair!"

"When I come back, we'll start over. You might meet someone new and decide it's too much work to repair us and it would be easier to start over. I won't hold it against you. You are a beautiful woman, I won't stand in your way."

My heart was breaking and he didn't even care. I wanted to curse him out and lash out at him, but that wasn't going to change anything or make me feel any better. I walked out of his apartment and I told my heart to let it go. My heart screamed at me. I told myself I had a week to fall apart and then I had to get over this. I had to move on.

Ahjani

I couldn't sleep, every time I fell asleep my subconscious screamed at me for letting Olivia leave. When I couldn't take it anymore I looked at the clock. It was almost four, I called Olivia and she answered immediately. I asked her if I could come over. She said yes without any hesitation. When I got there, her eyes were swollen and puffy. She had on sweats and her hair was in a bun. It was probably driving her crazy. I wouldn't doubt that she thought about cutting it all off again. "I can't sleep!"

"Ok."

"Everything is crazy. I love you, I don't know what to do."

"Love me, make love to me, let everything else go!"

"It's that simple?"

"When you want it to be, anything is that simple."

"Olivia I'm going through something. I don't know if it's even fair to take you along on this trip."

"Ahjani I want to go anywhere you want me to go."

"Why? Who does that?"

"I am in love with you beyond all comprehension. I don't want you to leave me behind. Did I misunderstand; was that night your way of telling me you wanted to have a baby? Cause...."

"NO! I wanted to get back in, didn't want to waste time talking." She exhaled. "You want a family now?"

"No! But if you wanted it, I'd change our plan."

"You love me that much?"

"I can't breathe without you. I don't know how I lasted that long without you, but I can't go on without you."

I watched her eyes as she spoke from her heart. "I love you Olive, but I'm..."

"Ahjani just tell me what to do, and I will do it."

"Can you come out to California at some point?"

"Of course!" She walked in her room. I heard her flip the switch to turn her computer on. She had her work calendar out. "Is it ok if I come back and forth for the preexisting gigs?"

I told her to stand up, then I hugged her. There are moments that you never forget. When you notice a woman for more than just her physical attributes. The moment you realize you're in love with said woman. The moment when you will never know a woman who loves you more than the one you're looking at.

Olivia

"Did Paula say whether she needed you to come in daily while I'm out?"

"As long as she can reach me by cell, she said it's fine." Julia put the baby on her hip. "So, Spencer is graduating this month."

"Un Huh!"

"It's going to be up in the air where he's going to live right now. His father wants him to come home, and he's trying to convince him of why he needs to open an office out here. Me and the baby will have to move to whatever city he settles in."

"No, Jules! They're trying to separate us." I smiled and touched the baby's chin.

"Liv be serious. I'm telling you that I may end up moving away."

"I understand, what would be holding you here?"

"Duh! You! You moved across the country to be with me."

"I know, but it's not like I'm not going to follow Ahjani where ever he ends up. Whether we go back to California or anywhere he needs to go."

"What if things don't work out for you and Ahjani, you'll be out here alone."

"Julia, I'm a big girl. I know how to pack up and run back to Royal. I'll be ok."

"You'll have to come out and visit me, no matter where I end up."

I hesitated, "stay with you and Spencer?"

"Girl please! I'm getting my own condo wherever we go. He's just my baby's daddy."

"That you're in love with?" I watched her eyes.

"That ship has sailed." She said in defeat. "I just want to do what's right for Julian. I could meet someone and my life will be complete."

"Yes you could."

"Anyways, I just thought you should know." She put her diaper bag on her shoulder.

"You need a ride?"

"No, Spencer sent a car service for me. I'll see you when you come back." I kissed her cheek and then she left.

I told myself to knock off after an hour, but that hour quickly turned into two. What can I say, when you love what you do time flies. Suddenly Spencer was tapping on my open door. I screamed cause last I knew I was alone. "How did you get in here?"

He held up Julia's key. "She left Julian's blanket. You know how that boy won't sleep without it."

"Ok," I said returning my eyes to my computer as I internally screamed. This was bad! This was all bad! Paula's out of town. Ahjani's out of town. Julia has no car and is home! BAD! BAD! BAD!

"I finished school."

"So I heard, congratulations." I didn't raise my eyes.

"You're going to try to pretend that your pictures are that important, that you can't look at me?"

I glanced at him and then I looked back at my computer. "Leave me alone Spencer. You like messing with me."

"You don't bite off of hints, I have to be direct with you."

I squinted my eyes at him, "so what are you supposed to be doing? Besides causing me stress. I don't want Ahjani thinking I did anything to provoke you. All you did is transfer your feelings for Courtney on to me. This whole setup is faulty and just **WRONG**! You have a son with my best friend, you sleep with my boss. The only reason I even know who you are is because my man trusted you enough to bring you around. A lot of good that did him." I shook my head.

"I liked you before Courtney acted a fool, why you think you two were always doubling with us? I fell in love with you on our walks. You..." Then he rushed me.

I knew he was going to do this! Electricity shot up my leg and I started kicking cause this kiss went on and on. I turned my face and he started kissing the side of my face and my neck. "Stop it Spencer! If you loved me you wouldn't hurt me like this!" I said catching my breath.

"Livy please! Please!" Then he started kissing on my neck.

I slid out of my chair and onto the floor under my desk. I grabbed my chair and pulled it in. I would not let him pull the chair out. "Stop it Spencer! I will not compromise what I have with Ahjani for lust with you. You can have anyone you want, leave me alone!"

He got on the floor and looked at me, "anyone but you?"

"Right! I think it's just because you can't have me that you want me so much. I don't think you actually want me."

"Please come out! We will never have a moment like this again."

"I want to let the moment pass."

"Livy you love me too."

"Of course I do. You're Julian's father, but it's not the kind of love you're talking about."

"So every time I kiss you, why do you kiss me back?"

"I don't know, what else am I supposed to do when you're shoving your tongue down my throat?"

"Please come out, if you come out I will not kiss you unless you want me to."

My legs were getting cramped and my back was going to scream at me if I stayed bent over like this too much longer. "You promise?"

"I swear!"

"If you go back on this I will never trust you again!"

"I understand." He said as he slowly pulled my chair out. He sat in the chair and took my hands to help me up. When I started to walk away he squeezed my hands. "Sit." He motioned for me to sit on my desk. So I did, then I crossed my ankles. "Good day to wear a dress huh." He laughed at me.

"What Spencer?"

"Julia said she told you that I may move away."

"Right, and that she and the baby are going to follow you."

"My job like your job can be stationed from anywhere. I wanna be wherever you are."

"OH MY GOD! STOP IT SPENCER! Leave me alone!"

He chuckled, "Lubbock doesn't even see you. You talk about someone who's rebounding and you point at me. He's the one, you can't even see it. The problem is that when I tell you I love you, you know I'm telling you the truth. When I kiss you, you know it comes from my heart. I'm not saying Lubbock doesn't love you, and everyone knows you love him. I need you to understand that he's not the only man who will love you. He's not the only man to appreciate you. If I would have known that he was going to lose sight of the precious jewel he has in front of him, I would've drove home that night. I would've let Paula pine after me. He's normally a very smart guy."

"So why not let him hang himself. Why do you keep doing this?"

"Because I know that you will think that you have to put up with it." He looked at me, "I can't sit back and watch you hurt and act like I don't see it."

"Ahjani makes me happy, and he's who I want."

"And I want you."

"And Julia wants you."

"See how the cycle continues. I think it should at least stop at me and you." Then he smiled at me.

"You're cute Spencer, but I love my man."

He exhaled, "ok so kiss me goodbye and I'll go back to my son."

I shook my head, "then you'll throw it in Ahjani's face."

"Livy, I want to be with you. If I ever told that would jeopardize everything. I will never tell a living soul that we were here alone together. I want you to kiss me at least once."

My heart tells me that Ahjani's been with someone else. Perhaps it's the Nellie girl who's name he says in his sleep sometimes. He says her name and he says mine, no other names. I told Spencer to come to me and I kissed him. My leg started shaking, it only does that with him. His hands went everywhere and settled under my dress.

When I got home I thought I would cry or feel horrible. I sat in silence and I asked myself what did I just do?

****

"How come he's come home every summer, and you're here sporadically?" Royal asked.

"My job has me all over the place. Ahjani only works during the summer."

Royal listened but it's not like I convinced him. Ahjani's brother called him asking where he was cause he wanted to see him. Royal invited Aunrey over for dinner with us. I sat over to the side watching them talk and have a good time. I needed to do something so I started cleaning up. Ahjani came in the kitchen and put his arms around me. "You coming with me tonight?"

"I am never having sex with you in your mother's house again." I whispered.

"The only person who would've heard us is Audra and she's not there. Come on, you know you want the excitement as much as I do." He smiled, I didn't. He laughed, "I was going to get us a room."

"I'm kind of tired."

"When has that ever mattered?" He kissed me. "It's time for you to purr for me. I think this kitty is overdue for some catnip." When I made a purring sound at him, he rubbed my back and said "good kitty. Now go get your coat."

****

"I didn't sleep with him." I said embarrassed.

"Aw! That's so sweet. So you did like the teenagers and petted each other. How cute!"

"Don't tease me."

"What did he say afterwards?"

"He made me promise that when Ahjani messes up that I would come to him. I told him Ahjani wasn't messing up, but he wasn't listening to me."

Paula gave me a yeah-right look, funny thing is. I guess I don't believe it so much anymore either.

Ahjani
This summer has been bitter sweet. Seeing Nellie again was great, but her brother made sure he stayed just about planted in our conversation the whole time. It's like suddenly there's a barb wired fence around her. No one's getting in no matter who they are. When I asked her why she left ASU, she wouldn't give me a straight answer. She just said she couldn't be that far away from home any longer. I wanted to hold her, kiss her. But her family stayed around and she didn't want to leave the house. It was like she was happy to see me, but only to a point.

Then Olive looks guilty, what's going on with these women? Can somebody please be straight with me and stop playing these games?

Chapter 12

Olivia

Everything is weird now. Julia and the baby followed Spencer to Detroit. The times that she calls me when Spencer is there her tone is weird and she sounds irritated. But I guess that's because he's all in our conversation and he won't get out of it. She talks to me for a while and then she gets off the phone. I guess he makes her call me, cause I wouldn't call anyone again if Ahjani acted like that in the background.

Before they left, the looks Spencer would give me would make me want to run and hide. He would almost smile at me and then he'd look like he was remembering the uncharacteristic night here at the studio with me. I was afraid that he was going to act more sprung or something, but it's like he's holding his breath if that makes any sense. Like I gave him just enough to get some act right and now he's waiting. He did come to me and ask me to kiss him goodbye though. When I hesitated he said he didn't know when he would see me again. Kissing Ahjani is always good, but for some reason I only get that feeling in my leg when I kiss Spencer. So I sucked it up and actually enjoyed my last kiss with Spencer. He touched my lips and said as soon as it is confirmed and I was free I needed to call him. He gave me his number and then he left.

Sometimes I think Julia wants to ask me if anything happened between Spencer and I, but she talks herself out of it. We talk about how big Julian is getting. She emails me weekly pictures of my baby along with all of his nuances for the week. Spencer bought her a condo and she doesn't have to work. She says she takes care of Julian and when Spencer feels like being bothered with her, he breaks her off. She sounds so unhappy and I feel sorry for her. I don't know what else to say.
Paula has moved on to her next boy toy. This one is even cuter than Spencer. Paula says she doesn't know how long he's supposed to last though cause he's actually catching feelings.

Ahjani.... he's kind of been all over the place. Agents are coming all the time trying to get him to sign with them. His game has been on point, and it seems like every game he plays win or lose more and more people raise their heads and notice him as if they hadn't noticed him before. More and even bolder groupies come from all over trying to get his attention. At first I wondered if he slipped up with a groupie, but Ahjani is never interested. It's to the point now that when he meets with agents he wants me there, and it's like he's saying this is my woman, don't offer me sex. Crass I know, but when it becomes the reoccurring theme you get tired of the politically correct stance.

Now, Ahjani asks me questions and then he waits and watches my face like there's some secret that's going to spill out. I don't know what he thinks, but I tell myself not to volunteer until he does.

****

"Lubbock has the free throw down to a science." SWISH! The crowd goes wild! I cheered him on like I normally do. I was in to the game as people were entering my row as usual, but I was focused on Ahjani and blowing him my usual kisses whenever he looks at me. His cologne and her perfume were strong. They invaded my nose and choked me. I slowly turned my head to the left in disbelief. It was…. my parents! I frowned at them…… together? And all the way out here? Ms. Roth shot me a look like I better not act up or she'd get me. "How's he doing?" Mr. Evans said smiling from ear to ear as he looked out on the court.

Fire turned inside of me. I couldn't believe the nerve of these two idiots to actually come here. I scooted a seat over and tried my best to go back to watching the game. Ahjani frowned at my mom and then he went back to his game. At the end of the game Ahjani's team lost by three points at the last minute. The ball barely cleared the net and I was up and walking to my right to get out of this row. Ms. Roth watched me while she spoke to Mr. Evans. As I waited outside of the locker room they approached me. "You know it's very rude to walk away from your parents like that. I know I raised you better than that," Ms. Roth said.

Mr. Evans stood there smiling like this was some kind of blissful and happy family reunion. "Lubbock is amazing, I wouldn't be surprised if he went in the first round of the draft pick."

Ahjani came out focused on my face. "Ms. Roth." His tone was dry.

"Ahjani this is Olivia's father Dr. Landon Evans, say hello." She commanded.

Ahjani frowned at her, "it's so nice to finally meet the young man who's captured my little girl's heart."

Shock was all over my face, when was I ever his little girl? Ahjani put his arm around me. "Dr. Evans, thank you for coming. We're going to leave now. You two have a nice evening."

"And where do you think you're going?" Ms. Roth said.

"I don't know what kind of game you're playing. Seeing how upset Olivia is by your presence I don't care to know. I'm taking her home, thank you for coming and supporting the game but I cannot be a part of whatever you two have going on here." Then he took me out of there.

I tried to act like I was ok, and like the fact that I knew my parents were out here and together didn't bother me. When Ahjani got in my bed he told me to stop pretending and to let it out. I cried my eyes out in his arms. They didn't even care about me or how they affected me. They only came because my boyfriend was about to be someone huge, not because they cared anything about me.

****

"Can you move your arm a little more to the left?" I directed my model. "Good! I like those eyes! Yes more like that!" Normally Paula has critiques throughout the course of my shoots, but today she watched silently. "Can you move that light a little more to the left?" I asked one of the crewmembers. I kept looking at Paula to make sure she was ok. I was shooting for a fashion magazine in New York. They loved most of my pictures for the last fashion week, and they invited Paula and I specifically.

When we left the location Paula smiled really big at me. I asked her what was on her mind, and she kept smiling and shaking her head. We had dinner at this Korean fusion place in Manhattan near our hotel.

Paula put her hand on mine, "you were amazing today. There wasn't anything I would've done differently on that shoot."

I smiled from the inside out, "thank you Paula. That means a lot coming from you."

Then she sat up straight, "but that's also why you can't work for me anymore."

"What?" I felt like she shot me.

She looked at my expression and then she laughed, "calm down. I'm offering you a partnership. Eventually I'm going to want to retire all my lenses. I can't be your boss anymore. I think we should be partners."

"Paula!" I put my hand up to my mouth to cover it cause I immediately fell into the ugly face cry.

She chuckled at me, "calm down. Do you always have to be the girl?" She tried to pretend like she didn't want to join my tears.

I could barely talk, "you have no idea what your friendship, your mentorship, your everything has meant to me. Knowing you has changed my life."

Paula took a deep breath like she was trying to reign in her emotions, "You have reminded me why love and passion are important. I've gotten so used to not having it in my life, I thought I learned how to live without it."

"Paula!" I touched her hand.

"Stop it! You're turning me into this sappy crybaby. Cut it out!" She dabbed her face with her napkin. "We'll go over everything with a lawyer ok? I'm so excited for you. For us!"

Ahjani

My off schedule visit home was chaotic, it was supposed to be great. People got shot, houses got shot up. Jason was angry beyond belief. This guy named Bobby from North Richmond defied all sense of right and wrong and came against the wrong family. Jason and Aunrey refused to let me come with them. They made me stay behind and make sure that my sister and cousins were taken care of. They said I couldn't afford to be with them and something tragic happened. So yeah, somehow I was supposed to be ok with being the whimp of our family. I wanted vengeance for my family just like they did. I was just as angry and upset as they were, especially when this Bobby cat was the reason for Nellie's pain. Lots of bodies fell in North Richmond that night. Once again I was close to Nellie and then circumstances pulled us apart. When I could actually get her on the phone she was too upset to talk. When I went by her house a guy with a long ponytail went up to the front door. I tried to tell myself he was a family member, but he wasn't black, I knew he had to be Marquez. I wanted to be there for her, but right now she didn't have capacity for me. So I focused on Kendra who was pretty heartbroken about everything. When she asked me to go to the hospital with her to see Omar, I was hesitant because I really wanted to hurt him. He was the reason Nellie was holding me back, and this fool wasn't cherishing her. He wasn't appreciating her for everything she is. I did not feel sorry for him laying up in that hospital bed. I did not feel sorry for him and the loss of his career. I told myself not to be this dumb.

****

"Hello?" I didn't recognize this 510 area code calling my cell phone.

"Ahjani Lubbock?"

"Who is this?"

"This is Doctor Evans." He said like I was supposed to be grateful to talk to him.

"What do you need?"

"I wanted to talk to you about my daughter."

"I wasn't aware that you had one."

"I guess I deserve that."

"You guess?" What did he mean he "guess?"

"Look, I'm not calling you to get a lecture from a kid on stuff you know nothing about. I'm…"

"Why are you calling me then? Olivia wants nothing to do with you. You were out of line for showing up out here like you did. I don't know how a girl that great came from such beastly parents."

"Look! I don't want to hear all that. I want to offer you your first endorsement deal. I want you to endorse my laser eye care facility and I will pay you handsomely for it. Money is money!"

"You want me to endorse you and I'm not even Pro yet?"

"We all know you're going, and when you go you won't be riding the bench either. I would like to be your first endorsement deal. We can negotiate pricing."

"Don't call me again! But I want you to think about this. If you had been even halfway decent to your daughter, I would've gladly done it for free!" Then I hung up.

****

It was all over the television that I was going to play in Miami. Jason sent out lawyers to help me go over my pretty standard contracts and the few perks available to me as such. My momma cried, my family told me how proud they were for me.

119

Olivia cried with excited tears for me. I looked at her with excitement and contentment.

****

My house wasn't big and it wasn't fancy, four bedrooms and three bathrooms. It's in a nice and gated community. My family came out to help us paint, and finally Olivia got to run free and decorate like she's always wanted to. When I tried to put them on a budget Olivia bucked my budget and said she had money. Olive, my mom, sister, and Auntie ran to the store laughing wickedly.

I kept getting frustrated cause I got no real cell reception in this house. Olive said it was because my phone was ancient and in desperate need of an upgrade. She took me to the mall and I picked out a fancy phone like she had. This phone had so many bells and whistles I told myself I needed to sit down with the owner's manual and really give it a good look over. I kept butt and pocket dialing people. Olive joked that when she realizes that I've butt dialed her she listens for the sound of another woman's voice. Things are going really good for us right now. There are a lot of new things for us. I wish I could stop my heart from looking back though.

Olivia

HUMIDITY! UGH! GASP! PANT! I am a California girl. When it's hot it's just hot. "Dry Heat" I guess is what you would call it. The humidity is bad in Georgia, but nothing beats Florida. I hate it, but my stupid stinking hair loves it! In the past few months my hair has grown like they were harvesting it in a lab or something.

Meeting these actual Basketball wives is something else. Some of them work, and others consider their jobs as girlfriends and wives as full time work. Ahjani and I look at those few as poster children for what not to do. The rest are really nice and welcoming. Paula and her tag along boy toy came out while Ahjani was in training. She said that Ahjani seemed a little off.

I would've been worried about it, but the other day he butt dialed me while he was having a man to man conversation with one of his teammates. They were talking about groupies. The teammate was saying how difficult it is to resist and Ahjani told him there was nothing a groupie could offer him that would ever make him want to risk what we had. I was so touched by the conversation that I wondered if he set the whole thing up so I would somehow accidentally hear them. When Ahjani came home he was normal, he didn't mention his conversation or act like he was looking for me to mention it. Later that night when we were fooling around his mom called and told him to put his phone up cause he kept butt dialing her. I screamed and ran away!

I explained to Paula that Ahjani was focused and getting his mind in the game. She gave me a knowing look like she knew as well as I did that there was more to that look than just that.

****

"I fly out first thing in the morning. I'll go to the hotel rest up a bit, then I'll make my way to the stadium."

"So we won't link up until after the game, that's fine." Ahjani was excited and happy, happier than he's been in a minute. "I'm going to link up with Kendra and Ahjanae, take my momma out to dinner. You know the standard routine."

"Ok, I love you, and I can't wait to see you."

"I love you too Olive, talk to you later."

When we hung up, I had a smile on my face and everything was right with the world. A few minutes later Ahjani was calling me again. When he didn't respond to my hello, I listened as usual.

Ahjani

"I'm here can you meet me?"

"You're where?" Nellie sounded surprised.

"Oakland, we're playing them tomorrow. I need to see you." She hesitated like she was going to try to give me some kind of excuse for why she couldn't come out. So I told her I was coming over. There was no way she wasn't seeing me today. When we hung up the phone I put my phone on the inside pocket of my jacket. I sang along with the radio, I played an imaginary drum. I felt good and seeing Nellie was going to make me feel better. When she opened the door her perfume greeted me first, I swept her up and squeezed her tight. I told her that I missed her so much. Her little sister was sitting in the chair looking like a gorgeous preteen. I gave her a hug when the glimpse of the bling of Nellie's ring caught my attention. Fire and disappointment ran through my body. "WHAT IS THAT?"

"We need to talk," she patted the couch for me to sit.

"Let's go!" I pointed to the door.

She shook her head, "no. It has to be here, and Nassya lovingly agreed to stay in the room." Her little sister smiled then she put her headphones on. She busied herself with homework.

I looked at her sister then her. I know that everything that happened was traumatic, but did she actually think I would ever hurt her? "You think I'm going to hurt you?"

"No, I know I don't need to fear you. I can't trust myself when it comes to you."

"Trust yourself? That's real?" I pointed to her ring." You're marrying someone who isn't me?" I couldn't believe it. "I don't understand Nellie! It's me! We're in love! You can't possibly love whoever he is more than you love me!"

"Come on, you're in love with Olivia and you question me?"

"I don't love her more than I love you! I've always loved you first!"

"She's your girlfriend, if I was truly first you would've broke up with her as soon as you found me. Marquez loves me, I'm first with him. He knows everything about me and he still loves me."

"I still love you!"

"You don't know everything! You could never be here for me like Marquez is."

I kissed her lips, "Nellie don't! Don't marry him! I'll marry you! We could go right now, I have the rest of the day off."

"And then what? Olivia's lovingly waiting for you to return to her. Why would you hurt her like that? She doesn't deserve that kind of pain. Be good to her Ahjani, you are not that guy."

She was giving me way too much credit. "Nellie!" I put my head between her breasts. "My first love! Please! Don't do this!" I continued pleading with her trying to help her see my point. "I hate your father! He should've left us alone!" I wanted to find Mr. Parker and beat him until his heart was bleeding like mine. I spent another thirty minutes pleading with everything in me for this woman to choose me. Again! She didn't choose me. I could see the struggle within her to deny me, which is why I kept pleading. Alas, I got tired of hearing my own voice. I walked out in disbelief. I sat in the car for a few minutes trying to grab my composure. Nellie really rejected me, fell on the sword for Olivia. I took out my phone to call Ahjanae cause I needed sisterly advice on whether to give up. When I took out my phone there was already a call in progress. The timer on the call said it was quickly approaching an hour. The caller ID said that it was Olive, my heart sunk. "Hello?"

She was crying on her end of the line, then she hung up.

Chapter 13

Olivia

Now what? I couldn't come up with a complete thought! I called Paula and I couldn't talk I was crying so hard. She asked me questions and I just kept crying and crying. She knew by my cry that it was Ahjani. She convinced me to go online switch my flight out to tonight, to go to Miami get my things and then come to her place. I caught the last flight out. I walked in his house feeling so defeated. This was no longer our house that I happily made a home. This was his house. I only took the things that mattered like all my clothes minus all the pink stuff. I put everything in my car. Then I went in the bathroom. I actually didn't mind my hair longer now that I've learned to wear it curly. But this down my back stuff has to go. I put my hair in a ponytail; I looked at my hair and took a deep breath. Then I cut it off just above the ponytail holder, my fallen hair felt so final. I left the severed hair on the bathroom sink since he loved it so much. I thought about trashing his place, but I knew that was just my bleeding heart. I got in my car and cried as I drove ten hours all the way back to Georgia. Paula hugged me and I cried my eyes out in her arms.

I told her I couldn't hear everything or understand everything he was saying. But I heard him declare his love for her. I heard him beg her to marry him, and his offer to marry her on the spot. She weakly refused him the whole time. At least now I know who he was sleeping with.

Ahjani

I don't even know what to do. Ahjanae and Kendra went off on me so badly. When I tried to argue my case they had a response for everything I said. No matter how I tried to spin it there was no escaping how badly I messed up. In the matter of an hour I lost the two women who have meant the most to me ever.

I had an amazing game though. I was on my flight bright and early directly home. I planned to plead with Olive for forgiveness. I mean I've forgiven her; she could forgive me, right? Her car wasn't in the garage, but she could've gone to the store. I told myself to stop being stupid. It looked like a pink explosion on her side of the closet. She left every pink item she owns it looked like. Even in the drawers, the only things in them were pink. I felt like she punched me when I saw the hair on the counter. To be funny I told myself she could turn this hair into a weave and sew it back in. I called her cell and it went straight to voicemail. So I left a message. Every hour I left a new message. I was just rambling really, I didn't know what I was trying to say. I just knew I needed to apologize.

Olivia

When I turned my phone on, my phone broke out in a seizure as it vibrated and signaled that my mailbox was full, something that's never happened. They were all messages from Ahjani. I stood in the mirror looking at myself trying to get a grip as Ahjani rambled on and on not saying anything that mattered to me. I took most of my clothes, which were mostly the way Ahjani liked me to dress, and I donated them. I made an appointment to get my hair fixed.

When I walked in the door my stylist's mouth fell open. She hurried to me and hugged me, which made me cry. She knew I was growing my hair for Ahjani and all that he meant to me. She made me cry again and I had finally stopped crying. When I sat in her chair she asked me with big eyes what I wanted to do. I told her that I wanted my curls to hit my shoulders. I needed her to clean up my chop and give me some shape.

Then I went shopping. My Grays, Browns, Blacks, Dark Purples and Navy Blues were my colors of choice. On the lighter side I did get some Khaki colors, Olive Greens, and creams. As I picked out my things I realized I was breathing again. How many years had I been holding my breath? I bought mostly black underwear sets, since they were mostly pinks and all for Ahjani before, I barely had any to bring.

When I got home I showed Paula everything I bought. She smiled at my choices; she was quiet mostly listening though. Probably cause my mouth had a mind of its own. I kept talking cause every time I stopped talking I'd start crying and I was over crying.

Ahjani

"Olive! This is the millionth message I've left you! Please call me back! Baby, I'm sorry! Please talk to me! Cry at me or something! This silence is too loud I can't take it! Please Olive!" I put the phone down and then I looked at the machine. I hit play again and I sat there watching me make love to my Olive. I smelled my fingers as if her smell would still be there. I put her pillow under my nose and inhaled trying to convince myself that she was still here. I needed my Olive here in the worse way. My game has been great! Sponsors are noticing me; my agent is calling me with endorsement deals. I go out sometimes, but I always bring my own car. I always leave early, groupies aren't my scene.

I took a deep breath, "hello." I could hear the smile in her voice.

"Are you busy? I need to talk."

She hesitated, and then she excused herself. "I kind of knew you'd call."

"Nellie I messed up! Olivia heard everything." She gasped, "She won't take my calls. I'm pretty sure she went back to Georgia. But, I don't even know what to say to her. She heard everything."

"Oh Ahjani! I'm so sorry! Blame it all on me."

"Why?"

"Why not? You're trying to get her back aren't you?"

I exhaled, "yes... I guess!"

"Don't be dumb! You love her! You were perfectly happy with her before you found me again."

"Almost, I was trying to make her be you. She loved me so much that she went along with it."

"I see. What made her..."

"Why are you choosing him over me? I was here first!" I surprised myself with my anger.

"Ahjani I will always love you. It's just that if you truly knew me you wouldn't feel the same."

"Everything you're talking about is in the past."

"Why would I harp on your past?"

"Because it affects my future. You don't know Ahjani. I'm completely messed up, I could never be the woman Olivia has been to you."

"You don't know what we've gone through."

126

"I know that everyone loves her, and that you two deserve to be together. Ahjani stop being stubborn. I can't be with you! I've promised Marquez with all my heart, you wouldn't try to make me out as a liar."

"I don't care about him! I'm talking about me and you!"

"Ahjani, this isn't you. I'm sorry for the part I've played in all of this, but I will not end up like my parents. Maybe you can't see it, but I do. No amount of love will ever make me volunteer to live like that. You don't see it. I want to be able to see you and smile, but if you can't understand that I cannot and will not be with you then I have nothing else to say to you."

Anger filled my stomach, "if I'm asking you to be my wife how are you reliving your parents?"

"Because you won't realize until I need you that you're really in love with Olivia! We were kids! You have no idea who I am now! You know and chose Olivia as an adult. I'm sorry if you don't get it Ahjani! I love you, but I will NEVER be with you!" Then she hung up.

Olivia

I told myself to smile and get through it. Another Millionaire, and his Bridezilla wedding. This bride is the worst! She screams at her bridesmaids, she was screaming at her grandmother for crying out loud. You should've seen the way she looked at me when she opened the door. She didn't say hello, or introduce herself. She wanted to know why I was dressed like I was here for her engagement photos. I told her I couldn't wear a dress and capture all the photos she had on her list. I was going to be squatting and everything else. A dress was not a practical choice. Then I started snapping. She immediately turned on her smiles and poses. The way I captured her you would think she was the sweetest person ever. Once I was finished inside the house I went outside to setup for the ceremony. I talked to the videographer to confirm his line of sight, things like that. Then I saw him; he walked to me with one hand in his pocket. His eyes bounced over me and then he smiled. He came in for a hug. "Livy," then he said in my ear. "You were supposed to call me."

How does he know? "Why?"

"You're a free woman, I can see it all over you."

"Is Julia here?" I looked around.

"No," he watched my eyes.

"Ok, well the ceremony is going to start soon. It was good seeing you." I said hurrying to my spot.

Spencer took his place in the audience, and his eyes stayed glued to me. I centered myself then I focused on my job. I captured beautiful pictures of their ceremony, and the post ceremony pictures at sunset were beautiful. Spencer stood over to the side watching the entire time. So much for me slipping out of here quietly. When our pictures were finished the groom thanked Spencer for suggesting me. Spencer stayed close by all night. Julia says that she's over him; she even has a boyfriend now. I still don't feel good about any of this. When some big about business looking man was talking to Spencer I took that as my cue to run! I packed up the last pieces of my equipment and I quickly walked out to my rental car. I thanked the bride and I told her I'd send her a couple of the negatives in a week. I got in my car and I drove away as I saw Spencer walking out the front. I stopped at a store and I got a bottle of Vodka, a bottle of Kahlua, and a quart of vanilla ice cream. My ice cream barely fit in the tiny little freezer, but I made it fit. I sat on the bed trying to get a hold over my nerves, and wait to see if Spencer showed up. Of course he'd show up now, I don't know how I feel. Ahjani only calls maybe once a month now. I should've changed my number like he did to me. When I felt the coast was clear I got in the shower and washed my hair. I put products in it and slicked it down for the night. I put on my processing cap, and face cream. When room service brought my burger I got comfortable in the middle of my bed. I enjoyed my meal while I watched a movie. I'd never seen it before and it was doing a good job of keeping my attention. I made a tunnel type hole in the middle of the carton of ice cream. I filled it with vodka and Kahlua, every time my well ran dry, I filled it back up. My private shameful ritual. I almost screamed when my room phone rang. It was the front desk and they said a Nicholas Spencer was requesting that they call me for him. I told the guy to give him the phone. "Hello."

"Go away Spencer! I'm very comfortable in my room alone."

"I've seen you comfortable before, I was at Paula's house in the mornings. Please let me up, I only want to talk." He laughed.

"Yea right!"

"Oh come on! I've been driving around trying to find your hotel."

Vodka! Vodka! Vodka! "Fine! I'm in room 385."

"See you in a minute."

I ran to my suitcase. I grabbed my bra and underwear, and then I hurriedly put on my sweats. He was just going to have to deal with the processing cap and face cream. He knocked on the door sooner than I was ready for him. I told him to wait while I moved the shame from the middle of my bed to the desk. I picked up my tossed clothes and then I took a deep breath and opened my door. Spencer smiled really big at me and then he hugged me as I let him in. He laid his trench coat on the chair and then he took his shoes off. I told him to get comfortable sarcastically; he said he was trying to get on my level. He sat on the bed with a big goofy smile. He told me to tell him what happened. I shook my head; I said I wasn't in the mood for "I told you so's!" His smile went away, he asked me if I was ok. I shook my head no. He got up and he put his arms around me. I've been missing the touch of a man, but I stayed guarded. I asked him how Julia was doing and he said she's fine. He told me she has a boyfriend, he said he doesn't like it, but what could he do about it? We chatted and I watched the clock show me that it was getting later and later. I told him I bought a Loft back home in the Bay. He excitedly said his brother is out in the Bay, and he'd have to come visit. He asked what I was drinking, I took everything out and then he shared my spoon as we proceeded to finish the carton. We were laughing then my alarm went off on my phone saying it was time to head to the airport. I don't remember falling asleep. Spencer was still fully dressed as he tried to wake up. I left the small remainder of my alcohol in the room. Spencer followed me to the airport. I gave him my number and I thanked him for being a friend last night. He slowly pulled me in for a kiss; I guess he was waiting for me to object. When I didn't, he kissed me and there it was, that electricity. As soon as I got to my gate he called me. We talked until I boarded my plane.

Ahjani

"How come I haven't seen or talked to Olivia?" My momma asked.

I had been avoiding this for as long as I could. I exhaled and prepared myself for my momma to smack me upside my head. "We broke up."

"What?" She smacked me just like I knew she would. "What did you do?"

"Why does it have to be me? Why couldn't it have been her?" She glared at me. I sunk in my seat. "She heard me propose to Nellie."

"Nellie? Where the? Why?" I could see her getting mad. "That Nellie girl has too many issues! You saw what happened all because of her. I guess her parents figured since she's grown now they don't have to honor my wishes anymore! That girl...."

I couldn't believe my ears, I cut her off. "Your wishes? Your wishes? You're the reason why?"

"I told her parents to keep her away. She had too many issues."

"Momma!" Air burned in my chest. "You're the one who broke my heart? You're the reason I've been walking around here broken?"

"Ahjani, she had too much going on."

"You were so busy meddling in my business that you forgot to keep an eye on Ahjanae, or get a hold on Aunrey! Momma how could you break my heart like that?"

"I was doing what I thought was right."

"You're the one!" I sunk in my chair. "Why couldn't you have paid more attention, but let us run our course? Spared everybody this pain."

"What if I did that and that Bobby guy found you, he would've killed my baby for nonsense. You could've ended up like Omar."

"Omar got what he deserved, you don't even know momma."

"I did what I knew was right in my heart. And now you need to get over the past and get my baby back!"
****

He stood as the host showed me to our table. I chose this restaurant cause it was a delicious little hole in the wall restaurant off Gilman street on the out skirts of Berkeley and Albany. It was after the morning rush and before the lunch rush. It was so empty in here at the moment that there was only one other table with two people at it. He didn't let the nonchalant expression on my face rob him of his smile. "Ahjani! It's good to see you!" My father said.

"Ahmad," I said acknowledging him.

"I watch all your games, I'm so proud of you."

"Would you be so proud of me if I was pushing paper in someone's office? Or if I became a dentist like I wanted and may still do."

"Of course! Are you proud of Ahjanae? Have you met your grandchildren?"

"She had more?"

"Exactly!" I exhaled, "I didn't come here for you to kiss my converse. I need to say what I need to say and then I'm done." I looked at him, "I really hate you! Because of your lack of interest in us outside of drama, my sister went looking for love in the wrong places. Ahjanae is with a good guy now, but she's in constant fear of being left behind so she goes for things she shouldn't. You've never seen your granddaughter or your grandson. They're great kids and you don't know them. I had a good woman who bent over backwards to supply all my wants, because as long as I had her I didn't need anything. My momma did the best she could, but it's not natural for a woman to raise children on her own."

"It's not my fault your mom had all those kids!"

"How about the two you left her with? Two kids too many! It's no one's fault my father died."

"You mean stepfather."

"I mean FATHER! He stepped up when you weren't man enough!"

"This is why you invited me here?"

"Mostly, Ahjanae..." The host was showing Spencer and Olivia to a table. Olivia's hair was in a wild ponytail, black sweats that swallowed up her body, and no makeup. I took a deep breath. She didn't have an after sex glow, but that doesn't mean anything. What is she doing out here? I kept telling my eyes to look away but my rage was growing. I know I made this fool a promise, he must be testing me. I was trying to calm down but I couldn't. My rage kept growing until I was out of my seat and approaching them. Spencer's eyes finally looked at me when I was on them. I laid into his stupid pretty boy face. Olivia screamed cause she didn't know what was going on. The element of surprise was on my side and I took all my frustrations out on him.

"AHJANI?" Olivia screamed in surprise. "STOP IT PLEASE!"

"YOU WON'T ANSWER MY CALLS BECAUSE HE GOT YOUR EAR?"

"WHAT ARE YOU DOING HERE?" She ran to Spencer.

That made me mad again; I snatched Olivia by her arm as Ahmad ran to the table. "Take her out of here, I'll take care of this."

I pulled Olivia towards the door as she grabbed her purse and tried to fight back from me dragging her out of the restaurant. "Ahjani let me go! Please!"

"WHY? SO YOU CAN GO RUN BACK TO HIM? WHAT ARE YOU DOING HERE?"

"I live here!" She cried, "what are you doing here?"

I put her in the rental car. Then I hurried to the driver's seat. I was barely in the seat and I was driving off. "Why haven't you answered any of my calls or called me back?" Olivia stared at me as I drove with the evilest expression on her face. "ANSWER ME!"

"Answer you?" She hit me upside my head just like my momma does. "Answer you! IF YOU DON'T PULL THIS CAR OVER! I DON'T KNOW WHAT YOU THOUGHT, BUT I HAVE NOTHING TO SAY TO YOU!"

"We are not little kids, we can talk this out like adults. If we're not going to be together then we need to discuss it! You can't just leave me!"

"Yes I can! AND YES I DID! WERE YOU GOING TO TELL ME BEFORE OR AFTER YOUR HONEYMOON IF THAT GIRL WOULD'VE SAID YES!"

I looked at her; I drove to the Richmond Marina. I drove to the backside that overlooks the Bay. "Come on."

"No!"

"No?"

"NO! YOU'VE KIDNAPPED ME AND I WANT YOU TO TAKE ME TO MY CAR RIGHT NOW! I DON'T WANT TO BE HERE WITH YOU!" She crossed her arms.

I got out and opened her door, "please come." She folded her arms and refused. So I picked her up and took her out of the car. I carried her over to the side where the big rocks created the shoreline. I sat her on a big rock, and then I stood next to her. She refolded her arms and huffed. "Olive I am so sorry! This past year without you has been miserable for me. You have every right to hate me, I was wrong for everything. We never did have the conversation about our past relationships, or how our parents affect us. I could see you struggling so hard not to be the dragon lady. It took some thinking, but I understand it now. You flipped out on me that night because I was doing like I had always done. Thought about my gratification and what I wanted first. I wasn't treating you like a partner, I wasn't building with you. You knew it, and you loved me anyways. You compromised so much about who you are to be with me. Your hair, your clothes, everything about who you are, and I let you. I was afraid you were going to leave me. I was afraid you weren't going to love me after a while. The only person that I wanted to believe would love me had already moved on with her life. She grew past yesterday; I was the only person not growing. I love you Olive, I want you back. I don't care if you wear black all day and every day."

"What about if I shave my head like I planned to this afternoon?"

"None of that changes who you are. I don't care what you do with your hair."

"Are you done?"

I was wishing that my words had some kind of effect on her. I could see as clear as day that she had a shield around her heart, and my little heart felt speech wasn't going to win her over just like that. "Yes."

"Take me back to Spencer!"

I fought back the urge to choke her and dump her body in the Bay where no one would know. Instead I did as she asked. I drove around the corner, and then I watched her put Spencer in her car. I followed her to her loft in Emeryville. I wrote down the address, and then I started coming up with a plan.

Chapter 14

Olivia

That morning I went to the gym, then I picked Spencer up at the airport. We were going to have breakfast, and then hang out for the day. I had no plans of sleeping with Spencer, I still didn't feel comfortable. But then Ahjani comes out of NOWHERE acting completely unlike himself. Well not exactly unlike himself, cause I do remember him threatening Spencer before. I certainly didn't think he was capable of doing anything. I mean I knew he was capable, but I didn't think he'd do it. I didn't know he was out here, and what are the odds, that we'd end up at..... I felt horrible, I knew that spot was Ahjani's, he's the one who introduced me to it. But he's supposed to be living on the other side of the country. When Spencer finally calmed down, we had a good laugh about it. Ahjani came out of nowhere, Spencer wasn't even sure that he saw Ahjani cause everything happened so fast. Spencer said the old man helped him up and then he started telling him this big and animated story that had nothing to do with anything. Spencer said he was mad cause the old man did successfully distract him from his throbbing nose and lip. Spencer laid on my couch with frozen bags of corn on his face. Spencer joked that the fight would've been at least interesting if he even saw Ahjani coming. He sat up and asked me what Ahjani said to me. I glossed over his apology, it was all words to me anyways. It didn't matter what he said, I was done.

****

"Hello Ms. Evans, I'm calling on behalf of Torrie Rowe. One of her very good friends shared the pictures that you took of her engagement and wedding. Ms. Rowe would like to have you audition to do the photography for her upcoming album cover."

Torrie Rowe? Oh my goodness! Torrie Rowe wants to work with me!!!! I pulled it all back and tried to keep my composure. "That sounds good."

"Ms. Rowe is going to be shooting the first video for this album, and she'd like to invite you to audition by photographing her video shoot. There will be two other photographers there capturing pictures as well. Whoever captures the essence of the song and video the best will be awarded the opportunity to work with Ms. Rowe. Please give me your email address and I will send you all of the detailed information."

When we hung up I had a huge smile on my face. Spencer came out of the guest room ready to be dropped off at the Bart station. I offered to take him into the city for his meeting, but he asked for a ride to the Bart station instead. We were having dinner tonight at the Equinox restaurant in the city. This restaurant was at the top of a building and it slowly rotated. The city in all it's glory was the back drop to the delicious food there. We were supposed to have dinner with his brother who lives out here in the Bay; with everything that's happened he decided against it. He said his cousin was going through a divorce and he's pretty heartbroken about everything. Spencer said its pretty bad and his cousin has custody of the children. He thinks the soon to be ex-wife is in jail. I told him I applauded his cousin for stepping up for his children.

I took Spencer to the Bart station and then I hurried back to create my proposal for the shoot. I called Paula then we reviewed the proposal over a virtual live meeting online. Paula said she liked working with children and animals more than she liked working with most celebrities. She said some of them, not all of them, were real divas also known as big babies. Once we finished with the proposal and I sent it back. I told Paula about everything that happened yesterday. Paula warned me that Ahjani was going to try harder now that he's had my ear. I told her that Ahjani and I were never getting back together. Paula told me to never say never when it comes to matters of the heart.

I got dressed in a black dress, real shocker there, and then I made my way over to the city. Spencer and I had a lovely meal, the wine was flowing and his little battle scars were sexy. As we left the restaurant, Spencer kissed me the electricity shot through both of my legs kind of making them turn to jello. We walked hand in hand back to my car. I guess I could let this happen once at least; after all he did take a beating for me yesterday. When we got to my place we barely made it in the door we were kissing and touching. We went to my bedroom and Spencer laid me down. We were kissing for a long time, and eventually I asked him if everything was ok. He said yes then he went back to kissing me. He kissed me, he groped me, everything. When I reached towards his belt he backed away from me and then he put his forehead on mine. He looked embarrassed as he told me to give him a minute.

That's when I noticed that there was no tent in his pants. So we kissed some more, and for a long time. When his friend refused to show up no matter what, Spencer ate dessert, which he was very good at. I could tell the last few days were nothing but an embarrassment for him. He even tried in the morning and nothing, and he was beyond embarrassed cause nothing like this had ever happened to him before. Personally I think Ahjani had succeeded in hitting his mark when he emasculated Spencer in front of me.

****

When I got to the studio the music was already bumping. Torrie was very scantily clad leaving nothing to the imagination, as she danced around a guy with a nice body as he stood there letting her. The song was called, "If you were mine" and was basically Torrie trying to seduce a guy. When they yelled break the guy turned around and it was Ahjani. I wanted to scream! Did he have anything to do with this? What a coincidence that I got invited to be here right after he saw Spencer. Was this supposed to be his opportunity to show me that he could pull someone else as well? I watched the other two photographers hurry over to Torrie to introduce themselves. Torrie told them she didn't care who they were, and that they needed to bore her assistant with the details. Ahjani gave her an irritated look, and then he made small talk with the photographers. I could tell he felt bad for the way Torrie behaved. He engaged them in conversation and got them talking, he did a good job of smoothing out her rudeness. When they called them back to their marks, I could definitely see that Torrie was definitely feeling Ahjani, but by the look on his face he was not interested. Since he's a nice guy he was trying to let her down easily. I snapped pictures of them before the music started, when Torrie wasn't acting. When she was actually trying to get next to him. The director was giving Ahjani, who wasn't used to doing this sort of thing, direction. Ahjani posed for me before, but this was motion picture. As the director yelled action Ahjani saw me, the surprised expression on his face let me know he did not know I would be here let alone have anything to do with me being here. He would not take his eyes off of me, and I could feel the pores open on the top of my head as I tried to keep my cool and not let him see me sweat. Now the intrigued look that the director was looking for was there on his face. I wanted to scream and get out of there. Every time the director yelled "cut" Ahjani looked for me. I tried to make sure I was talking to the assistant or someone; I did not want to talk to him or be here. They did wardrobe changes, but I had already gotten the shots I needed. I hung around snapping more pictures just for the sake of seeming engaged, but I was over it.

"Good evening Little Miss Olive Oil." I didn't even notice that he was close to me.

"Hi," I didn't want to talk to him.

"I didn't know you were going to be here."

"I could tell."

"How?"

"Your eyes got four times bigger than their normal size."

He tried to smile, but I know his big eyes can be a sensitive subject for him. They never bothered me, and I thought they were quite beautiful before. I used to imagine that people would call our daughter Princess Jasmine behind the beauty of them. Right now I don't want him thinking that I'm open to the idea of him. "Honey! How much longer do you have?" Josephine said as she approached Ahjani.

Josephine was a tall, thin, and beautiful up and coming model from England. With her heels on she was the same height as Ahjani, and she paid me no attention. "We're almost done. Josephine this is Olivia, she's one of the photographers." Is that all I am? "Hello," I said holding my camera for dear life.

"Nice to meet you. Did you get any nice shots of my baby?" She asked me like she was hoping I'd share my photos with her.

"Your baby? Are you two dating?"

She smiled at Ahjani, and then she looked at me. "We don't want to announce it to the world yet, but we're getting there."

"Well you know after this video people are going to think that he's dating Torrie."

She rolled her eyes, "people can think whatever they want. Can you take some pictures of us together?" She threw her arms around Ahjani who did not look like he wanted to be there at that exact moment. I smiled at them and snapped away.

I was grateful when Torrie's assistant called me away. The assistant asked me to present my pictures within the next two days. I got in my rental car and flew to Georgia. Paula and her boy toy were having some kind of lovers quarrel by the front door. She was telling him to get out and he wanted to talk to her. Seeing Paula so unglued was alarming. I asked her what was wrong and she said he was cheating on her and she didn't have time for it. Then she looked embarrassed because her jealous rage meant she caught feelings for this guy. All this time she was trying to make it seem like it was all him. I gave them space to carry on and I got on the computer. Two hours passed before she finally came in her office where I was. Her face was sad and she looked exhausted, she said stuff like this is exactly why she'd rather not invest feelings. I asked her if he was gone, she hung her head and said no. I changed the subject by showing her my screen. She gasped when she saw Ahjani. In the most animated fashion I told her about my day. Before she came in I was secretly admiring the pictures of Ahjani where I cropped Torrie out of them. For most of the shoot he was shirtless in jeans, and that's the way he liked to walk around at home. I missed his body, and I missed making love to him, BUT I did not miss him! He betrayed me in the worst way. All I can think about is what if she would've said yes? How would he have explained to me that he married someone else? That's how Ms. Roth ended up married four times. Hanging out with her ex-husband, angry, and taking her frustrations out on me. I wonder what happened to the husband number five hopeful? I don't care!

Paula asked if Ahjani and I spoke as she stared at his pictures. "Um Paula? I know we're not together anymore, but I will cut you!" She laughed I didn't.

"Oh honey, he's beautiful! I don't know how you look at that screen and you don't slip back into yesterday. I know he hurt you, and you have every right to be upset. I just wonder if it's worth throwing it all away for?"

"I'M NOT THE ONE WHO THREW EVERYTHING AWAY! I'M NOT THE ONE WHO EVER WANTED US TO END EACH TIME IT WAS HIM! HE NEVER LOVED ME! HE WAS USING ME TO FILL THE VOID THAT GIRL LEFT!"

"Who is she?"

"Does it matter?"

"You can play not interested all you want. I wanna see her."

My curiosity was peaked, "how would you find her? I doubt her actual name is Nellie."

She smiled, "leave that to me."

****

"I can't believe I let you talk me into this!" My heart was pounding and I was irritated.

"Calm down! We'll interview her and then we can say we're done with this whole thing."

They stepped into the restaurant and immediately I knew it was her. She was average-tall, long dark almost black hair, bright pink pea coat, black boots, grey skirt, black shawl, pale gray blouse, GORGEOUS! There was a guy with her; he looks like he's from an island. He was very cute and mild looking. The host showed them to our table, even Paula's eyes bucked when she realized they were coming to our table. Her eyes were focused on Paula. Her friend nodded at me. "Hello Nealesha Parker, this is my fiancé Marquez." She smiled proudly.

"Nice to meet you, I'm Paula Giovinale and this is my partner..."

She cut her off when she saw me and her smile dropped. "Olivia? I guess you're the Evans in this partnership?"

Ok, now I feel like crap. "I wasn't aware that you knew who I was."

"Ahjani very proudly showed me your picture. A woman doesn't forget that look in a man's eyes." She watched me.

"Please have a seat." Paula gestured towards their chairs.

"We were very impressed with your website. We were thinking that your services were out of our league." Marquez said taking his seat.

Nellie openly looked me over the same way I was taking her in. "You want to ask me something." She watched my eyes.

"I don't want to disrespect your fiancé." I gestured towards Marquez.

Nellie grabbed his hand, "it's ok. I don't keep secrets from him about anything."

"Why did you break up?"

"Our parents kept us apart. We didn't technically breakup."

"Why did you reject his proposal? I heard you, and it sounded like there was a part of you that wanted to say yes."

"There was a part of me that wanted to say yes. Ahjani was the first to see even a piece of me. I do love him for everything

139

he's meant to me. He was always good to me. There are so many things he doesn't know about me that I could never expect him to understand and still see me in the same light. I'm convinced that no one could love me like this man right here." She glanced at Marquez with love in her eyes. "Besides, I couldn't get past how much he loves you. I'm too selfish to be patient about you living in his heart."

"You think he loves me even though he proposed to you?"

"That was an impulsive move. The true romantic nature of him choking out reason and logic."

"He's a romantic guy?" Marquez asked with a smile.

"I told you, you must've forgotten..."

"Or blocked it out." Marquez smiled.

"You two haven't gotten back together yet?"

"No! I'm not getting back with him. What if you would've said yes?"

"He's in love with you, I was his first puppy love experience. Sometimes those experiences are hard to let go of because of the fact they were what opened our eyes to those new feelings. He met you when he was ready to settle down. You are a better match and fit for him than I could ever be. I don't know him like you do, and he loves you on a level I only know with this man. I understand being upset about what happened, but Ahjani is a good guy. He messed up royally, make him pay, but don't count him out. I don't wish that kind of life on him especially when I know how much he loves you. And you wear love for him in your eyes."

Paula looked at me, "she does doesn't she."

I frowned and looked away. "Marquez, what would you do?"

He smiled, whipping his gorgeous smile at me. I bucked my eyes at Nellie cause her man immediately became delicious and I wasn't expecting that. "I believe in standing by the one you love until you're absolutely done. I don't know too many people who approach love the way I do."

Nellie gently touched his face, and he melted a little. "Baby you are unique. I love you so much being that way." Then she gave him a quick closed mouth kiss.

He smiled at her as he bit his lip, I looked at Paula. She picked up her menu and started fanning herself. "You stinking kids!" We all laughed. "Now that, that's out of the way. We invited you here because we wanted to feel you out and get a close look at you. If we didn't like you we were going to quote you our normal prices. But now having met, you are your delectably tasty man, I'd like to do your engagement photos as a gift, and I'll extremely discount your wedding photos and do it myself."

"Oh My God!" Nellie said like she just won the lottery. "Thank you so much!" She kept touching Marquez and he was eating it up.

I didn't want to, but I found myself liking her. I wanted to hate her guts, but she didn't want Ahjani so I guess I could let it go. Paula exchanged information with them. She was going to do their shoots; my part in all of this was done.

Ahjani

It is not my fault that the Evans & Giovinale site lists their itinerary for the next six weeks. Orchids are coming to Olive's place weekly. Singing telegrams will pop up randomly when she's out.

I reached out to Torrie's assistant and asked who they decided to go with for Torrie's cover. She said Torrie told her to pick and she wasn't sure. So I told her to choose Olivia. She sent me the pictures that all three photographers submitted. The other two's pictures were nice. Olivia's main picture made me stare. I know I was irritated with Torrie, but this picture made it look like she was actually succeeding in seducing me. I wondered if she thought I was into Torrie and then Josephine shows up. Josephine likes to go everywhere so we'll be seen and linked together. She gets so excited when she sees us together on the headlines. I like quiet evenings at home. She likes to go out. She turned purple one night cause I didn't want to go out. She doesn't like having sex, so we really have nothing in common. But I digress... The assistant said she didn't care one way or another. She started venting about how much Torrie pisses her off. Her tangent was completely unprofessional, but completely entertaining. I told her I would love to come to the shoot to see her go off on Torrie. Her assistant was so done! She sent the offer letter to Olivia while we spoke. She sounded surprised when she got Olivia's immediate acceptance. So I told the assistant I needed to level with her. I told her that I needed to be as close to Olivia as possible. I gave her the story in shades of red and gray. By the end of our conversation we had a plan built around Torrie's photo shoot.

****

My plane arrived an hour before Olivia's. I waited in the limo nervous that she would try to run as soon as she saw me. Olivia's hair was loose and her curls were bouncing with every step, she didn't shave her head. She quickly got in the limo and threw her bag down before she realized I was there. She cursed when she saw me. "Stop sending me flowers and having crazy people jump out of bushes randomly singing old school R&B at me! It's creepy and not funny!"

"Hello Olive Oil how are you?" She huffed and turned her body towards the window. I moved closer to her, and she sucked her teeth. "Olive, we're going to be stuck in this Southern California traffic for a while. Go ahead, tell me about it."

I expected her to yell, scream, and make my ears bleed. "You broke my heart Ahjani." She said with so much pain in her voice.

I wanted to cry, "Olive I'm so sorry!"

"You're only sorry cause she said no. You wouldn't have cared about me or my feelings."

I put my arms around her. I waited for her to tell me to let her go, but she was crying too hard to say anything. "Please don't get mad at me for being honest. You're right, at first I would've been happy that she said yes. But in my mind I would've expected her to think and act like you. Thank God she was smart enough to reject me. Nobody compares to you."

She cried harder, "stop touching me! I'm with Spencer!"

I wanted to choke her again. I was quiet for a minute. "Ok, but he's not me."

"That's right, he doesn't care how I wear my hair, what types or color clothes I wear, he accepts me and appreciates me for who I am."

"You said you were going to shave your head. I believed you, and I still kept trying to win you back, I don't care about your hair."

"You still prefer long hair though!"

"That's my personal preference. Just like you prefer men with big ole girl butts. I'm sorry if I got a little nice booty."

Olive stopped breathing then she busted out laughing. "Stop talking about Spencer like that."

"I'm saying just because big booty is your preference it didn't stop you from loving my little booty."

"I used to love you, I don't anymore."

"I'll take it, as long as you don't deny we had something." I kept my arms around her. "So how you been?"

"What do you think?"

"I'm thinking you had to be feeling good at some point to let Spencer in."

"Don't act like you care now. You would've been off into la la land with Nellie, you wouldn't have cared."

"I will always care about you."

"You can say that now because she turned you down. I thought I told you to stop touching me."

"Come on Olive, the last time I held you is the last time I got to exist like this. Please let me have this." When she didn't respond, I knew I needed to keep her talking. "How's Julian?"

Her mood lifted, "he's getting so big." She showed me picture after picture on her phone. When we pulled up to the hotel I kissed her cheek, then I released her. The concierge greeted us at the door and the bellhop loaded our luggage and followed us. He took us to the fifth floor and then he gave us our keys. Our rooms were side by side. Olivia opened her door and music came pouring out as the singing messengers sang a Jodeci song begging for forgiveness for me. Olivia jumped so hard then she screamed my name telling me to cut it out! She kicked the singers out. I chuckled to myself as she fussed about the life size picture of me standing by her bed. I tipped the bellhop and concierge as they stood there trying not to laugh at the scene. Olivia slammed her door. I opened my door to her room then I knocked on hers. She snatched her door open holding the cutout of me. "For real?"

I rushed her and kissed her.

I had my hands in her hair massaging her head. "I'm sorry Olive, forgive me!"

She almost melted then she took a step back and slammed the door. I moved just in time to miss the door slamming shut.

Olivia

I HATE HIM! I HATE HIM! I HATE HIM! If one more person walks up to me and starts singing I'm gonna snap. Why would it be funny to get on my nerves? I locked the adjoining door and then I pushed the desk across the room in front of the door. Then I ordered room service, but in order to get my meal I had to endure another song. Ugh! I hit the door and imagined him laughing. He knocked on the door and I ignored him. I turned his life size picture towards the wall. I called Paula and she seemed to think something was funny about the whole setup. She asked me if Ahjani looked good. I was quiet, and then I told her he did. She told me to at least get a tune up since Spencer failed to do the job. Then she laughed harder. She said she couldn't believe he didn't show up and that they never had that problem. There was no way I could let Ahjani in even for maintenance. I knew he'd turn me out again and I'd be bent over backwards apologizing to him for everything.

That night I had a dream that Ahjani and I made up and then he put it on me so hard I woke up cause I was nutting in my sleep. That was crazy! If that desk wasn't still in front of that door I would've sworn he snuck in my room and messed with me in my sleep.

I got up, pulled my hair in a slick bun, my black cargo pants, black V-neck T-shirt, and brown camera bag. They called my room when my car service was downstairs. I expected to see Ahjani downstairs, but he didn't show up at all during the shoot.

I had a sinking feeling that idiots were going to keep jumping out at me every step of the way back to my room. I got all the pictures I needed and I even had to check myself cause I had no idea Torrie was such a jerk. Her assistant would smile real big at her and then mumble. I would be afraid she was stealing my money. If you're treating a person badly and they're always nice and never call you on it.... They're stealing from you! At least in my limited experience. When Torrie left in her thunderous fashion her assistant exhaled like she was so happy she was gone. Then she looked at me and smiled. She gave me two boxes. One was more rectangle shaped and white. And the other was square and black. The white box had long stem roses in it. The black box had a black dress in it that I left at Paula's. THAT TRAITOR! Ahjani hand wrote in a card begging me to have dinner with him. I took a deep breath. The assistant kept lifting to her tiptoes with excitement. "This has been my happy thought all day. You're going right?" When I looked like I was going to decline she grabbed my shoulders. "You don't say no to this! He's a good man and he's gone through a lot to be here like that. He loves you and he's fine! SAY YES!" She shook me, "SAY YES!"

"You don't know me!"

"What's to know? He loves you! He wants you! The rest of us are waiting to be noticed and you have someone moving the world just to be next to you. If you don't want him I'll gladly take him." She folded her arms as she let her sincere statement settle in.

I huffed then I got in the car. My shoes and jewelry were in there.

Ahjani

Around mid-morning I made way back to the airport. I met Paula at the baggage claim. She took the black box and the black bag out of her suitcase. She gave me motherly protective eyes as she handed them over. "If you mess this up I will hurt you!"

"I'm not worried about your threats."

"She still loves you, don't mess this up."

I held the limo door open for her, then I got in. "So she got with Spencer to spite me?"

The corners of her mouth turned up wickedly, "is that what she told you?"

My heart sped up, "it's not true?"

"My daughter's not a liar."

I clasped my hands together, "oh please Ms. Paula! Please help me. I was going to call the whole thing off."

She exhaled, "I'm only helping you so that you can give my poor child her much deserved happily ever after."

"Deal!" I leaned forward.

She exhaled, "she swears she's over you and she doesn't want you back. I'm telling you to continue like you have been."

"Ok, but is she with Spencer?"

"Why would you care about Spencer? You're Ahjani!" Then she smiled.

I waited for more but she didn't offer any more. So I had to sit back and check myself. Spencer is a pretty boy, but Olivia is in love with me. He was born with money, mine is growing steadily. Spencer slept with her best friend, mother figure, HOW COULD SHE BE WITH HIM? Why did I even fall for that? I gave my box, Paula's, and the black bag to the assistant; my partner in crime. I introduced Paula as Olive's momma. The assistant looked at Paula with stars in her eyes as she said "WOW!"

Paula checked in then she asked who was paying for these rooms when she came down. I told her Torrie Rowe. She laughed as she said that's why she signs all of her own checks. We spent the afternoon talking, but I knew she was checking to make sure I was sincere. When she saw Olive go upstairs she said she had to get ready and she'd see me in a little bit.

Olivia

I showered, washed my hair and diffused it. My hair obeyed and curled perfectly. Once I was dressed I opened my door and the assistant was waiting. She smiled really big at me, and then she told me to follow her. She opened the door and the room was just about covered in red with black and gold accents. Ahjani was standing in the middle of the floor in a black suit. The harpist played something pretty as I walked to Ahjani. Paula stood over to the side with a goofy grin as she snapped pictures of me. He took my hand and kissed it as he told me I looked beautiful. I took in the room; everything was beautiful. Ahjani asked me to dance with him while the waiters brought in our salads. Seeing Paula did help me to relax a lot. Paula and the assistant had dinner with us. Alcohol was flowing and the food was delicious. Everything felt like old times and I found myself getting caught up in the ambiance of the room. Well the ambiance of the room, whisky sours, and the handsomeness of Ahjani. Eventually Paula and the assistant left Ahjani and I alone. We enjoyed each other's company talking and talking. I let Ahjani kiss me then I told him the truth that I didn't know how to feel about him. I told him the first thing I felt when I looked at him was hurt and sadness. He shook his head and said he could understand that, he's been there. I asked him how he got over it. He said I reminded him of what was ***guaranteed***. His words turned my body into a flame. "Goodnight Ahjani." Then I went in my room.

Ahjani

I stood there feeling confused. Everything said she wanted me, but I'm standing in this hallway alone. I went in my room literally scratching my head. I took a shower and I let the water beat me in the face. When I came out of the shower she was standing in the middle of my room looking around like she was debating with herself. I walked up to her and kissed her. I told her, "I'm never letting go of you again!"

"You promise?"

"I PROMISE!"

MORE FROM THE AUTHOR

Thank you for allowing me to entertain you. I hope you have enjoyed reading my current release. If you have not read Volumes I – VIII of the Wallace Family Affairs series, please do so. Click here for a list of all the background stories. Once you have read the background stories, please checkout the current date series Together We Are Strong. Stay tune for more to come shortly.

Wallace Family Affairs
At Last (Click here)
Tracy's Complications (Click here)
Distorted Mirrors (Click here)
Sometimes Love Isn't Enough (Click here)
Love Is Just Enough (Click here)
Just A Friend (Click here)
Invisible (Click here)
Look Beyond Your Eyes (Click here)
No Regrets (Click here)
First You Laugh Then You Cry (Click here)
A Heart That's Taken
Abandoned (Click here)
Last Words (Click here)

Together We Are Strong
Season 1 Present (Click here)
Beyond The Wallace's ~ I Knew You When (**TBD**)
Season 2 What Comes Next (Release **TBD**)

Standalones
Secrets & Lies ~ (**TBD late 2016 release**)
Anthology **Short** Story (Where Love May Find You Collection) ~ (Click here)
Waiting (**TBD**)

Hopefully you've enjoyed all of the background stories for our lovely Wallace's and Latour's. Please tune in for more from the "Together We Are Strong" Wallace & Latour Family Episodes on Amazon.